slan*t*

Also by Laura E. Williams

Behind the Bedroom Wall
The Spider's Web
The Executioner's Daughter
The Ghost Stallion
Up a Creek

slan*t*

slant

Laura E. Williams

MILKWEED
EDITIONS

The characters and events in this book are fictitious. Any similarity to real persons, living or dead, is coincidental and not intended by the author.

Published 2008 by Milkweed Editions
Printed in Canada
Cover design by Jeenee Lee
Cover photo by Punchstock
Interior design by Dorie McClelland
The text of this book is set in Plantin.
08 09 10 11 12 5 4 3 2 1
First Edition

Please turn to the back of this book for a list of the sustaining funders of Milkweed Editions.

Library of Congress Cataloging-in-Publication Data

Williams, Laura E.
    Slant / Laura E. Williams. — 1st ed.
       p. cm.
    Summary: Thirteen-year-old Lauren, a Korean-American adoptee, is tired of being called "slant" and "gook," and longs to have plastic surgery on her eyes, but when her father finds out about her wish—and a long-kept secret about her mother's death is revealed—Lauren starts to question some of her own assumptions.
    ISBN 978-1-57131-681-3 (hardcover : alk. paper)—ISBN 978-1-57131-682-0 (pbk. : alk. paper)
    [1. Self-acceptance—Fiction. 2. Self-confidence—Fiction. 3. Adoption—Fiction.
4. Korean Americans—Fiction. 5. Single-parent families—Fiction. 6. Surgery, Plastic—Fiction.] I. Title.
    PZ7.W666584Sl 2008
    [Fic]--dc22
                                        2008007093

This book is printed on acid-free, recycled (100 percent post consumer waste) paper.

This book is for my BFF's
for always being there . . .
L.C.
C.C.
N.L.
P.L.
S.M.

Thanks to all the wonderful people
at Milkweed Editions for helping me
make a difference.

Thanks also to Sally, Charles,
and Bill for wanting and loving
such a crazy, diverse, amazing
family.

on*e*

It'd be nice if the wish I'm making on the thirteen candles I'm blowing out right now would come true. But like wishing on a star, I don't have much faith that blowing out a bunch of burning wax sticks stuck into a pink frosted cake will do much of anything. Then again, it doesn't stop me from trying.

"What did you wish for?" my best friend asks. Her name's Julie and she's rich and tall. "A cute guy?" she adds without waiting for my reply. "An A+ in math? A cruise to the Bahamas?"

"All of that," I say. The thing about lying is that no one knows it's a lie unless you get caught. Besides, if I told Julie my real wish, it'd never come true. I mean, that's how wishes work, right?

"Open your presents!" my little sister begs with one finger in the frosting, another one up her nose. When Maia is excited, her eyes fold nearly shut. Chinese eyes. I have Korean eyes. Everyone thinks we look exactly alike.

"Can I?" Maia begs, practically tearing the purple paper off the small box.

"Cease and desist, you rapscallion," Daddy says, taking the half-unwrapped gift out of Maia's sticky fingers. He hands me the package with a grin. "I believe this belongs to thee, m'lady."

Daddy talks like that a lot. He likes to say *forsooth* and *doth* and *take thee to a nunnery*—whatever that means. Because he teaches Shakespeare at Trinity he thinks he should talk old-fashioned. At least I think that's why he talks that way. Or maybe he's just plain psycho. He didn't always talk like that. But even when he was "normal," Mom used to say it was a good thing I was adopted so I couldn't inherit any of his weirdo genes. I think she was really kidding.

"Thanks, Daddy," I say. The card is half ripped-off, but I see *Lady Lauren* written across it. Gee, I wonder who it's from. I open the envelope. The card isn't as dorky as I expected. It's not of an out-of-focus girl running across a field full of flowers or anything. Actually, it's kinda cute with a cartoon of a dark-haired girl throwing confetti into the air.

Her boobs are bigger than mine, though. On the inside, he signed it *Love, Sir Daddy.*

I turn the envelope upside down, but it's surprisingly empty. I'm not looking for money. I'm looking for one of Daddy's long-winded notes.

I jiggle the gift box next to my ear. "What could it be?" I ask, even though I have a strong suspicion.

Daddy doesn't say anything, and his big Adam's apple bobs in his neck like he's got a fish on the line. I really hope he's not going to get all emotional on me. Jiminy Cricket legs, it's just my birthday. Okay, so I'm finally a teenager, but so what? It's not like I have anything growing on my chest (or under my arms, for that matter) to prove it! I don't even have my period yet.

Carefully I peel off the rest of the wrapping paper. Maia is slobbering with excitement, jumping on me, getting her face in mine. We sure don't need a pet dog with her around. Julie, my blonde, very-well-endowed-and-looks-like-a-model-and-has-had-her-period-for-months best friend is grinning.

I take my time picking off the tape on the four edges of the box. It's not that I'm not interested in getting this present, it's just that what I really, really want doesn't come in a box.

Finally I lift off the lid. Julie *oohs* and *ahs* at the pierced earrings. Maia grabs the next present. So much for a five-year-old's attention span.

"Thank you, Daddy," I say. I go around the table and give him a big hug.

Tears are there, glimmering behind his glasses. "Me thinks our little lady hath grown up," he says in a choked voice. Sounds like he has a lisp to me, but I don't ruin the moment with a sarcastic crack.

"Our little lady," he repeats, shaking his head.

I'm not supposed to say hate, but I really do despise it when he says *our*. There is no more *our*. Half of the *our* died three years ago. Why can't he accept that, change his lingo, and move on? Like I have. I don't say *my parents* any more; I say *my father*.

I give *my father* a kiss on his scratchy cheek and he wraps an arm around me for a quick squeeze.

I return to my seat, still admiring the earrings. For an old guy, he did a pretty good job picking out the perfect pair, and *finally* I'll have pierced ears like all the other girls at school.

Now I open Julie's gift to me. "It's totally awesome," I say when I get the lid off the large box. I shake out the purple suede jacket.

"Try it on," Julie says.

Giggling, I shove my arms through the satin-lined sleeves. It fits perfectly, just like when I tried it on at the store. I whirl in a circle. My straight-as-a-stick black hair whips around and half of it ends up in my mouth when I stop, dizzy.

"That's a very generous gift," Daddy says, frowning a bit.

"She's my best friend," Julie says. They eye each other. Julie's almost as tall as Daddy, even when they're sitting down, and I guess she wins the staring contest 'cause Daddy looks away first.

"Check out the pockets," Julie hints.

I do and I find a pair of black suede gloves. "Wow," I gasp. "They're awesome, too." I pull them on. I hold out my hands, admiring the fancy stitching on the backs and up each finger. I run around the table and give her a big hug.

"I want to open!" Maia shrieks. Both hands on another package, she rips the wrapping practically to shreds before anyone can stop her.

I take a flying lunge at the card as it sails by me. I miss. When I pick the envelope up off the floor, I recognize Grandma Milly's spidery handwriting. I open it.

> *Wishing you a day of happiness.*
> *May all your wishes come true.*
> [*Amen,* I add silently.]
> *Love, Grandma Milly and Grandpa Dick*

Daddy's parents. They live a whole fifteen minutes away. Too far to actually be here for my birthday party.

Maia almost has the present completely unwrapped. I grab it out of her hands and she squeals.

Julie rolls her eyes. She doesn't have a younger sister, just an older brother. Much older. Her parents are almost as old as my grandparents. Needless to say, she doesn't get this sibling stuff.

I finish tearing off the paper and find a picture frame made out of wood with painted pink roses all around it, but no picture inside. As pretty as it is, I know it'll sit empty on my wide windowsill just like all the others—all blank, looking at me, waiting for me to make a decision and give them faces.

One last envelope. It's come in the mail from Florida, so I know it's from Grandma Ann. Mom's mom.

The card is an embarrassment with bears tumbling across the front of it. I think they're Care Bears. Does she think I'm turning three or thirteen? Inside she's written me a note, which I read out loud.

Dearest Lauren,
I have a present for you, but I want to give it
to you in person. I'm arriving on Sunday for a
weeklong visit.
Can't wait to see you.
With love, Grandma Ann

I glance up at Daddy. He's looking a bit sick, but he's trying hard to smile.

"You know she's coming?" I say.

He nods. "Uh, yes. It'll be the greatest pleasure having her here."

Looks more like greatest *illness* to me, but I keep my mouth shut. Grandma Ann hasn't been for a visit since Mom's funeral. I picture a tall woman dressed in black. I think she always wore black, or dark blue anyway, like she was just waiting for someone to die.

"Is this a good thing?" Julie asks me.

"Is what a good thing?"

"Your grandmother's visit."

I shrug. "Sure," I say. "She's bringing a present, right? Heck, Jack the Ripper can come visit if he brings a present." I laugh a little to show how funny I am, then I cut the cake. Cake-in-mouth is a good way to stop all awkward conversation.

After my dad, Maia, and I pig out (Julie is on diet number 363, so she only has a bite), we all clear the table. Daddy offers to do the dishes, an added present for my birthday, and sends me off to walk Julie home.

Julie really doesn't need to be walked home. She only lives on the other side of our lawn, but I appreciate the chance to breathe some fresh air and look for a star. It's still early, but I manage to find one just barely bright enough to overcome the light of the setting sun. I make my wish. The thing about wishing for the same thing over and over again is that I know all the wishing words by heart.

We walk across the grass. Julie's house, or mansion, I should say, was the main house on an estate. We live in what used to be the servants' quarters. So once we walk across my lawn in like fifteen steps, Julie still has another thousand to go to get to her house. But we have a ritual. We only walk each other to the property line. Obviously Julie always has a longer walk than I do, but I tell her it's fair on account of her way-longer legs. One step for her is like three for me. Even so, it's still unfair, but I just tell her she could always have her chauffeur come pick her up. She usually shuts up after that. She says she hates being rich. Poor thing.

At the property line, we hug.

"I love my new coat," I say. I'm actually wearing it even though it's warm out.

"Nothing's too good for my best friend," she says back.

I watch her walk a little way, then she turns and waves before heading home at a jog. That's another thing she's good at. Exercise. Sometimes we stay after school and go to the gym together, when I'm in the mood for torture and shame. I'm not usually into those two things, so I mostly stay away.

I turn and walk back, my eyes lifted to the sky. More stars are out, but that first one I saw is still burning the brightest. I hope it's not a planet instead of a star. Wishing on a planet doesn't work, does it? Just in case, I pick another pinprick of light and wish on it too. I kinda worry, though, that this is negating my earlier wish since this really isn't the first star I've seen tonight. Have my two wishes canceled each other out? I comfort myself with the thought that at least I had my birthday wish. And a birthday wish, especially for a girl turning thirteen, should be pretty powerful. Not that I'm obsessed or anything.

When I get inside, it's time for Maia to take a bath and go to bed. She's pretty much covered with frosting.

"Come on, shrimp," I say, trying to avoid contact with her fingers. "Bath time." Lately this has become my responsibility, not that I mind. My father is teaching an extra class at the college this semester and is always overloaded with work.

I start the tub and she strips, wiggling and giggling and throwing her clothes around the bathroom. No modesty in her whatsoever. *Just wait till you're still flat at my age,* I think in her direction, *you won't go prancing around in your undies like that.* Then again, maybe she will. I remember that I was shy naked when I was little. Maybe when Maia is my age, she won't care about no boobs, no period, and slanty eyes.

I plop her in the tub and only get frosting up to my elbows. But when I reach into the water to rinse them off, Maia dumps a plastic cup of water and bubbles on my head. Shoulda seen that one coming. When will I ever learn? Wiping the dripping mess out of my eyes, I decide there's only one thing to do: It's time to call in the tickle monsters. The little brat has it coming to her.

Maia, shrieking with terror, and I, shrieking with menace, pretty much soak the entire bathroom in the next five minutes. Daddy only checks on us once.

"Rabble-rousers," he mutters and leaves us alone.

In the end, Maia is sparkling clean, and I look like a drowned rat, but we're both happy.

In her Barney pajamas, Maia is warm and cuddly. I love her so much my heart actually aches. And if it hurts this much to be a sister, I can't imagine how it must feel to be a mom or a dad. Of course, sometimes she makes me so mad (like when she takes my pointy markers and flattens the tips) or grosses me out (like when she eats her boogers), but sometimes, like now, I just want to gobble her up. I also want to warn her about her future. About the teasing and awkwardness and all the secret wishing. Or, better yet, keep her in her room where she'll be safe from it all. But I don't lock her up, and I don't say anything. Daddy might call this a *lie of omission*. Which means that keeping quiet about a truth is just as bad as telling someone an outright lie. He'd say it's wrong even if you don't get nabbed for it.

After she kisses Daddy good night, I put her to bed and get her favorite-of-all princess fairy books to read to her. Slowly, I read, pointing to the words like Mom used to do for me. I use all the different voices, even the deep, scary ones that might give a little kid nightmares. But Maia never gets them. She's braver than I am.

When she starts to suck her thumb, I know she's ready for sleep. I ease the book closed and kiss her on the forehead.

"See you in the funny papers," I say, just like Mom used to say to me.

Maia smiles sleepily.

I tiptoe out. It's still pretty early, but I'm tired myself. I find Daddy in his office, which is really the spare bedroom that he'll have to clean up when Grandma Ann comes to visit. He's correcting a pile of papers.

I put my arms around him, leaning against his bony back. "Good night," I say. "Thanks again for the beautiful earrings."

He turns on his swivel chair and pulls me onto his lap. "You're almost too big for this," he says, kissing my hair. "I can't believe you're a teenager." He sighs.

"I'll always be your little girl," I tease. I quickly kiss him good night and hurry to my room. If I don't, I know he'll start in with the *our* bit. Other than referring to me and Maia as *our children,* or whatever, he never talks about Mom. I try not to let that bug me, but I have to admit, secretly, that it does.

Anyway, it's time to go to bed. By the time I'm burrowing under my quilt, I'm half asleep. But not too asleep to do my nightly ritual. I'm not sure praying is any better than wishing on a star, but I figure with all the praying and wishing I'm doing, my dream is bound to come true sooner or later.

two

It's TTGLIFF. That stands for *Thank The Good Lord It's Finally Friday.* TGIF just seems too easy. And not only is it TTGLIFF, it's halfway through the day already.

I'm standing in the lunch line, following along behind Julie. She takes a salad. I take a double cheeseburger. She takes water. I take chocolate milk. She skips dessert. I never skip dessert.

It's not that I'm fat. I'm not. Some would even say that I'm petite. It's just that Julie looks at food and she gains weight. She pretty much hates me for my metabolism, and I hate her for her height, her wavy blonde hair, and her girl parts, so I figure I hate her more than she hates me. Funny how we're best friends.

We met when my family moved into the tiny house behind her mansion. We were both Maia's age now—five. The first time Julie saw me, she thought I was the gardener's granddaughter, and I thought she was a giant fairy. She really looked like one. You know, all fluffy pretty and wispy and wide-eyed, except she didn't have any wings. That didn't bother me, though. I figured she just kept them hidden under her shirt. So we got to be friends, her thinking I was one of the servants, and me thinking she was magic.

Someone behind me in the lunch line bumps into me. I turn around.

"Hey, chinko," says Greg. He pats me on the shoulder.

"Hi," I say.

His friend, Matt, says, "Yo, gook face, got any toothpicks to hold your eyes open?" They both crack up.

I kind of smile. What else can I do?

Julie whirls around and glares at the boys. "Don't talk to her like that," she says through perfectly even, white teeth. She's so tall she looks down on most guys.

"Oh, come on, bones," Matt says, still laughing, "we're only joking around." He looks at me. "Right?"

I nod. I want to escape. My burger's getting cold.

"Well it's not funny," Julie says. "And don't call

me bones, you little twerp." She pays the cashier, smacking her money down on the counter, and stomps away.

"Man, what rhymes with itch?" Greg says.

Matt opens his mouth. "Bi—"

The lunch lady gives him the evil eye, which only makes those two laugh even more.

I pay quickly and follow Julie to a table near the windows. She's still glaring as I sit down.

"Why do you let them talk to you like that?" she demands, picking up her plastic fork and wiping it on a napkin. She always does that.

I shrug. "It's no big deal," I say, wondering if Daddy would call this a *lie of submission*? I pour ketchup on my burger and squirt more out for my fries.

"It's racist and demeaning."

"They're just jerks," I say.

"That doesn't excuse them."

"They don't know any better."

"*You* don't know any better," Julie says.

"What do you mean, *me*?" I demand, sitting up straight. "I didn't do anything."

"Exactly!"

We don't speak again through the rest of lunch. It's lunch for me, it's picking through her salad for Julie. She doesn't eat anything that's a certain shade of green, so I don't know why she always gets a salad. Nothing green on a cheeseburger. She eyes mine hungrily, and I purposely make a show of enjoying a great big bite.

I'm on my chocolate pudding when Julie says, "So, do you still want me to come to the mall with you after school?"

I look up in surprise. "Of course."

She nods and stands up, tray in hand. "Fine. I'll see you in photography class."

"Okay, fine," I say.

"Well then, fine."

"Fine."

We smile at each other, still best friends. She waves and disappears into the throng of students who are clearing their tables, but she's so tall I can still see her blonde hair bobbing along in the sea of heads as she aims right for the door. I finish my pudding and join the crowds, letting the surge push me this way and that. It's easier to go with the flow than to shove against it. Luckily I'm pushed next to a garbage can where I dump my trash and deposit my tray. Unlike Julie, I'm so short I can't see a thing except shoulders and backs until I'm released into the hall and the press of bodies spreads out. Finally I can breathe again.

Until I see Sean O'Malley, that is. He takes my breath away, plain and simple. He's got reddish hair, too many freckles to count (though I wouldn't mind trying), hands big enough to practically palm a basketball (I admit they look a little goofy on him, but I figure he'll grow into them one day), and a smile that could melt an iceberg.

The only bad thing is the two guys on either side of him. Matt and Greg.

"Where's your bodyguard?" Greg says, looking around for Julie.

I smile. *Please,* I wish silently, *not now, not with him here.*

"So, slant, did you do your math homework?" Matt says.

So much for my wishes. Does that mean *none* of them will come true?

Sean frowns. I think he's going to say something to his friend about calling me names, but he only says, "Jeez, I forgot about that. I'm screwed." Knight in shining armor goes up in a puff of dust.

Matt's still waiting for an answer. I shake my head. I know he just wants to copy my homework. I should let him, and it'd serve him right. Does he think I get math just because I'm Asian? Maybe he thinks slanty eyes can see the numbers better or something.

"I'm getting a D in math," I say.

Matt hoots. "Yeah, right, and I'm the King of—of England." He turns to Greg. "They have kings there still, right?"

I marvel at the fact that when I actually tell the truth, I'm not believed anyway. What would Daddy call this? *A lie of disbelieving morons?*

I don't want to be late for my least favorite subject, so I step around the boys and head down the hall. I hear them following me. Well, not *following me* exactly, just walking in the same direction since we're all in the same class. I do wish Sean would follow me, like to the ends of the earth, or even just to my locker sometime, but no way am I going to waste wishes on that impossibility. Better to save them for something that might actually come true.

In the room, I sit at my assigned front-and-center seat. Maybe Mr. Driggs thought I'd be a good example to the other students. Maybe he thought I wouldn't be able to see over the top of anyone's head if I sat anywhere else. Maybe he went alphabetically—backwards, since my last name is Wallace. I don't dare try to figure out the last names of the two sitting on either side of me, just in case this theory doesn't pan out.

The bell rings, Mr. Driggs shuffles through the door, boredom sets in. Another typical math class.

Fifty-two minutes later, when the bell rings again (waking everyone up), I don't rush to the door with my classmates. I'll get crushed. Plus, I don't mind avoiding Greg and Matt when I can, even if it means missing a last glimpse of Sean. But to my amazement, Sean looks back at the last second before he disappears through the door, and he smiles. At me? I look all around. No one else here except Mr. Driggs. So for the rest of the day I have to wonder if that special, secret smile was for me or for the math teacher with the droopy pants, too much cologne, and a bald patch that I'm not sure he even knows about.

I make it to seventh period in a daze. Was the smile for me or Mr. Driggs? For me? Or Mr. Driggs? Mr. Driggs? Me?

"Hey, space-case."

My eyes focus. I'm about one inch from walking into Julie. We have photography together down in the art wing. Not that either one of us is artsy, but we had to sign up for some elective above and beyond our core curriculum, so we thought it'd be fun to take pictures together. I can't even draw a stick figure with a ruler, so I figured this'd be easy. You know, let the camera do the work. Ha!

After the first week of class, when Miss Shepard tried her best to teach us all the parts of a camera and explain about f-stop and shutter speed and other stuff I've already forgotten, she gave us our assignment.

"You are to get with a *partner*," she said.

Julie and I grinned at each other. Perfect!

"And take photos of *each other*."

This, I thought, was not so perfect. I hate having my photo taken. I'm so not photogenic. My nose looks flatter than ever, my eyes are slits, my hair is a black helmet.

"You are to capture the *essence* of the person you are shooting. Take a look at these photos by *Dorothea Lange*." She flashed a series of black-and-white images on the screen. "See how *Dorothea* captured the *souls* of these people during the *Depression*." She talks in italics a lot. She went on to explain how Dorothea Lange traveled across the United States during the Depression, shooting pictures of families looking for work and food.

One image appeared on the screen called "Migrant Mother." It was a picture of a woman with two children beside her. The children were hiding their faces. The mother had one hand to her face, and she was staring off into the distance. I was surprised to feel tears prickle the back of my eyes as I looked at this image. Another shot came up. It was another mother with two children. It looked like they were in a car or the back of a bus. She looked so confused, like she was wondering how she got there. And even though it looked like it might have been hot out, because the little boy wasn't wearing pants or shoes, they were all wearing heavy winter coats. I thought it was to remind them of when they had money, and I couldn't help wondering what their lives were like before the Depression, and where they went, and how they ended up . . .

Miss Shepard finished up with, "Use Dorothea Lange as your role model. Your photos must have *quality* and be *evocative, literary,* if you will. In other words, I *don't* want my-trip-to-the-Cape type photos. And you must not show your model the photos until the *end* of the quarter."

It's six weeks into the quarter now, and so far I have no evocative pictures of anything. They're not Julie's-trip-to-the-Cape photos. More like Julie's-trip-to-the-tree, Julie's-trip-to-the-couch, oh—here's a creative one, Julie's-trip-to-the-mirror. That was Julie looking in the mirror so that I got the back of her head and the reflection of her face. I thought it'd be so artsy and *"literary."* Mostly it was just out of focus because I didn't know whether to focus on her head or her reflection. The frame of the mirror is looking pretty good, but that's about it.

The biggest bummer about the class, other than having to have pictures taken of me, of course, is that we can't use digital cameras. Miss Shepard says we have to learn to really *feel* the camera and to *see* the image and to *experience* the chemicals and the *magic* of developing. I think it's just a way for the school to save money by not buying digital cameras. We use the school's ancient Canons.

We take turns in the classroom lab. Julie's signed up to develop film on Tuesdays and I'm in there on Thursdays. That's so we don't see each other's shots.

It's kind of an odd class because, unlike math where I get daily reminders of how poorly I'm doing, in photography we don't get a grade until the final week of the quarter when we all display our photos and get critiqued. I'm thinking that'd be a good week to have instant chicken pox or mono or the flu or something else contagious.

"Where should we shoot today?" Julie asks as I deposit my book bag on a table. She already has our cameras loaded with 200-speed black-and-white film.

"Does it really matter?" I say, taking a camera.

Julie gives me the stink-eye. "Of course it matters, but only if you want to pass this class," she says, like she is reading my mind.

"Okay, how about the caf?"

"Food pictures?" Julie wrinkles her nose.

"Then the gym," I suggest. This has a double benefit. I know Julie's into the gym scene, and I'm pretty sure Sean is there now.

"Great."

Oh, I'm so devious.

Julie grins at me as we walk down the hall. "You don't think *Sean* has gym this period, do you?"

Devious, *not*. Julie knows way too much about me.

I shrug like I don't have any idea and I don't care, but Julie just laughs and nudges me with her elbow. She does that a lot, and I have the bruises to prove it. Of course they're all up around my shoulder, seeing as she's a giant compared to my barely five feet of height.

We have to show our "art pass" to only one hall monitor. Miss Shepard lets us wander the school for location shots as long as we don't disrupt other classes, run in the hall, smoke in the bathroom, or get caught by the principal.

The gym is cavernous, which makes it loud and breezy. Only the breeze doesn't blow away the stink of rubber soles, "newly pubescent boys" (lingo care of Mrs. Flint, the health teacher) who haven't yet been turned on to deodorant, and the high-octane stench of Ms. Daniel's perfume. She's the gym teacher and kids call her Bertha Butt on account of her rather large rear end. I think she wears a bottle of perfume every day to cover the other odors, only it doesn't work that well. It's like eating a breath mint after a clove of garlic. All you get is minty garlic. Here the stink is perfumy B.O.

I'm still trying to decide what's the worst smell in this place, when I catch sight of Sean. Not that I was looking.

He doesn't see me, or if he does, he doesn't wave or smile. Now I'm sure his smile at the end of math must have been for Mr. Driggs and not me. Depression settles in.

"Sit over there," Julie says, waving me toward the bleachers.

I sit and ignore her as she walks and crouches all around me, clicking away. Mostly I just look away. I despise having my picture taken. I should have dropped out of this class. I hate it. Almost as much as I love Sean O'Malley, who likes Mr. Driggs, the drippiest teacher in the school, more than he likes me.

thre*e*

I *love* Sean? Yeah, right. How can I love someone
who obviously doesn't even know I exist? I'm
totally annoyed with myself.

"Nice face," Julie says as she clicks away.

I want to grab her camera and hurl it across
the gym, but throwing things isn't my strong suit.
I admit it: I throw like a girl, however sexist that
sounds. I'd probably make a fool out of myself.

It's time to go back to class. I take one last look
around the gym as we're heading for the large
double doors. There he is, looking right at me. I
think. He smiles and waves. I glance around for
Mr. Driggs. When I look back at Sean, he's walking toward the locker rooms, his back to me. On
impulse I raise my camera. No time to focus. Click.

"Come on, we're going to be late," Julie says, grabbing my arm. "You can flirt with your crush later."

"What? I wasn't flirting. And I don't have a crush on him! But do you think he was waving at me?" I'm such a contradiction I can barely stand myself. I know if Julie were carrying on like this about some boy, I'd probably have to dump her. How does she put up with me?

She rolls her big, blue eyes. See, Caucasians can do that. The eye rolls right around in a circle. Me, when I roll my eyes, they look like they just go back and forth. I know this because I've watched Maia try to roll her eyes. And even though hers are Chinese eyes and mine are Korean, the slant is very similar.

I suddenly realize I haven't taken a single shot of Julie all period. Yikes. Time to get busy. As we head back to class, I pose Julie next to a fire extinguisher, next to a poster for Just Say No, in front of the girl's room, in front of the boy's room with her hand on the door like she's about to enter (I kinda like that one). I shoot her walking from behind, her feet, from the front. Twenty-four—make that twenty-three—frames seems to be an awful lot. The second-to-last one I shoot up at her from the floor, as if I'm not short enough. I just hope something's in focus. I still don't get that f-stop business.

"Hurry up," Julie says, ruining my last shot by moving.

With a sigh, I crank the film back into the canister. I have to wait till next Thursday to develop it.

The bell clangs above our heads. I'm off to English, Julie to science.

"Out front after school, right?" she says as we exit left.

I nod. I have to hurry to make it from the art wing all the way up to the third floor for English. I zoom off, and I imagine my short legs churning like a cartoon character's.

Mrs. Hobbs is my English teacher. It seems kids have mean names for everyone, even the nicest, best teacher in the whole school. Hobo Hobbs, they call her, on account of her weird clothes. Nothing matches. Everything is patched. Her black men's shoes must be at least two sizes too large. Put a stick over her shoulder and she really would look like a hobo.

I'm panting by the time I get to room 313. In this class we were allowed to sit wherever we wanted at the beginning of the quarter. I sit front and center. Funny how that works.

I slip into my seat and Mrs. Hobbs smiles at me. Most of her face is as weathered as the side of a barn, but her hazel eyes sparkle like wet paint.

This is Advanced English. Mostly we read,

discuss themes and symbolism, and then write papers. In between she slips in sentence diagramming and vocabulary lists.

When we're reading novels and short stories and plays, Mrs. Hobbs doesn't tell us anything. She makes us figure out the deeper meanings for ourselves. Even after we think we've got it, she won't confirm whether we're right or wrong. She says it's all up to the individual reader.

Me, I love digging around, trying to figure out what the author was trying to say beyond the words she wrote down on the page. I'm like the symbol sleuth. The theme detective. The—

"What?" I say.

Mrs. Hobbs raises one bushy eyebrow and I can see she's trying not to smile. But when she's trying to look stern, somehow it makes her look even nicer.

"I asked if you have your paper," she says, her voice husky like she smokes five packs of cigarettes a day.

I quickly dig through my bag and hand over three typed sheets. I wrote about Romeo and Juliet's names in Shakespeare's play. About how Romeo Montague ends in weak vowels, and Juliet Capulet's name ends with a snapping consonant. I went on about how Juliet's name sounds stronger and how I feel Shakespeare wanted to show she's the stronger character. Three pages worth of proof.

Okay, I admit it: My dad helped me. He didn't

actually tell me what to write, but since he is a professor of English, specializing in Shakespeare, and I love that subject, we sometimes talk about it. He's always telling me how names can be very significant in a story, and he especially hinted about it when I told him we were reading *Romeo and Juliet.* But hey, what are dads for?

Mrs. Hobbs moves on with a swish. Somewhere on her body she wears a bell that tinkles every time she steps sideways. So far, no one's been able to figure out where the bell is hidden.

As Mrs. Hobbs makes her way between rows, some people start whispering. I press my fingers to my earlobes, feeling how smooth they are, with a little dimple on the backside. Will getting them pierced hurt?

Sandy, sitting beside me, leans over and says, "Is it getting too loud in here for you?"

I drop my hands onto the desk. "No, I wasn't plugging my ears, just wondering what it'll be like to have them pierced."

Sandy brushes her long hair away from her face. "You still don't have your ears pierced? I can't believe it. I had mine done before I was one. You're not chicken are you?"

"No," I say quickly. I pause. Which is worse, being chicken or having a father who didn't let me?

Luckily, Mrs. Hobbs has returned to the front of the room. Everyone knows not to talk when she's

standing there. It's not that she ever humiliates anyone into being quiet like Mr. Prescott, one of the
science teachers, or bores us into silence like Mr.
Driggs. It's just that even in her hobo clothes, she
somehow commands attention. We give it to her.

She puts her hands together like she's praying.
Large silver rings encircle each long finger, even
her thumbs. "Now that we've finished reading and
analyzing Shakespeare's masterpiece, it's time to
take it to the stage." Like a magician, she waves her
arms, as if that says it all. Somehow it does.

My heart starts to hammer. Stage? Not me, no
way.

"I will put you into groups of four, and you will
decide which scene to present. You have one week
to prepare your performances. Any questions?"

Someone in back raises a hand and asks, "Do we
all have to act, or can one of us be the, uh, back-
stage crew?"

"Really, Mr. Wilson," Mrs. Hobbs says (she calls
us by our last names when she's trying to make a
point), "I would think you'd jump at a chance to
perform. From what I hear, you're quite the actor."

A low *Ooooo* rises in the room.

"Slammed," someone whispers.

"In answer to your question, yes, everyone must
perform. Oh, and your lines must be memorized."

The previous *Ooooo* turns into an *Awwwww*.

Then comes the worst part. Mrs. Hobbs assigns

us into groups. My group is me, Sandy, Vanna, and Matt.

First thing Matt says is, "Hey, slant, you like this book?"

I know this is supposed to be *advanced* English, but maybe there was no more room in the remedial class. "It's a play, not a book," I say back.

"Looks like a book to me," Matt says, tossing the, well, *book form* of the play into the air.

Sandy looks at me. She's one of the most popular girls in school, if not *the* most popular. She's a cheerleader and her boyfriend is on the football team, of course. Talk about clichés. "Slant?" she says.

"It's her nickname," Matt says. He's serious.

I sit absolutely still so that I don't look like I'm squirming in my seat. I relax my face and open my eyes wider, as if that will help.

"Can we get started?" Vanna says. She has black hair and black nails, neither one of them natural. She looks like she might not have a brain on account of the occult or drugs, but she's really sharp. Rumor has it that Vanna only wears stuff from a secondhand shop she goes to every weekend in the Village. We're not too far from New York City, but my dad would still never let me take the train in by myself.

"Okay, what scene should we do?" Sandy asks, flipping through the pages.

"We have to use four characters," I say. "But I don't mind having a small part."

"Stand in line," Vanna says. She points to an open page near the end of the play. "How about this death scene? There's Romeo and Juliet and the friar and Balthasar."

Sandy looks at Matt. "You'll have to be Romeo."

"I'll be Balthasar," I say, remembering that that's the shortest part. And there's no way I'm kissing Matt, even if he is supposed to be dead.

"You can be Juliet," Vanna says to Sandy, "and I'll be the friar."

By the time we run through the scene (with Vanna giving us all tips on acting, on account of her seeing lots of off-off-Broadway plays), class is over. Yes, the weekend has begun!

I dash out of school with everyone else, trying not to get crushed in the throngs. I'm too excited to mind the body slams and flailing elbows. This weekend starts with having my ears pierced, going to a fancy-shmancy party Julie's parents are having tomorrow night, and finally picking up Grandma Ann on Sunday evening. I'm more nervous than excited about that last part, but I am curious to see Grandma Ann after so long.

I catch sight of Julie, or rather, Julie catches sight of me and hollers. I wave and wade in her direction.

"Excited?" she asks.

"Nah," I say, grinning up at her.

After we retrieve Maia from all-day kindergarten, we head to the mall. Even though we live out in a countrylike setting, a huge mall is only a fifteen-minute walk away along back roads, under the highway overpass, and over a mound of grass that once used to be a rubble pile from the building site (according to Daddy, who was actually a teenager when they built the mall).

Inside, there are at least five places I can have my ears pierced. I'd like to have it done in the back room where no one can see me, but Julie insists on this kiosk in the middle of the atrium.

"But everyone will see me," I protest.

"Yeah," Julie says, "look at *alllll* the people staring at you."

I look. We're like flies on the wall in Africa for all the notice we're getting.

"Okay." I give in. Besides, the girl working the kiosk is an older sister of someone on Julie's softball team, and she won't make us get a parent's signature and all that.

I hand over the twenty bucks my dad gave me this morning and choose a pair of gold studs. The loopy earrings Daddy gave me for my birthday will have to wait until I can take these out.

"Sit right here," the girl tells me.

I have to enter the kiosk and sit on this high, black chair. Now I'm sure I'm totally noticeable, but actually only Maia and Julie are paying any attention. Oh, and the girl about to jab holes in my ears. She'd better be paying attention!

Finally she says, "Are you ready?"

I hesitate. I've wanted pierced ears for how long? But it's going to hurt. I just know it's going to kill.

"She's ready," Julie says for me.

Yowch! But I don't say anything out loud.

Yowch again! My poor earlobes feel a little numb. I look in the small mirror the girl holds up for me. I have to tuck my hair behind my ears to actually see the small gold balls. Wow, they look— they look like small gold balls stuck to my earlobes. What did I expect? A miracle?

"You like them?" the girl asks.

"Yeah," I say. "Thanks."

"My turn, my turn!" Maia jumps up and down with excitement as I step out of the kiosk. "Me, me, me!"

"It hurts," I say.

"Okay," she says. I can tell she doesn't believe me anyway.

"Daddy won't like it," I say.

"But they're pretty," Maia says.

"Really?" I bend down so she can have a closer look. "You really think so?"

She nods. "I want to be pretty too."

That just about does it for me. Why shouldn't she be pretty? Why shouldn't she have something that makes her feel better about herself? I'll simply explain it to Daddy like that, I decide. Or maybe we'll just keep it a secret till she's thirteen.

"He'll kill you," Julie says to me. Sometimes I still think she's a very tall fairy with magical mind-reading powers.

"But it's what she wants," I say.

"She's only five," Julie points out, patting Maia on the head. "What does she know? She's just in kindergarten."

Personally, I don't remember much from kindergarten, but I do remember one thing. I remember being different. I was the only Korean. The only one with slanty eyes and hair as black as a crow's wing. Nowadays it seems like every other American couple adopts a cute Chinese girl, so Maia isn't the only one her age with slanty eyes. But still.

"Besides," I say out loud, as though Julie had asked, "Maia's old enough to choose her own ice cream flavor, so why can't she make a bigger choice? I mean, that's what growing up is, right? Making choices, making decisions!" Sounds like a good argument to me, and I may need it later if my wish ever does come true.

"Did I mention she's only in kindergarten?" Julie says.

"My turn?" Maia asks.

I look from Maia to Julie. "Can I borrow twenty bucks?"

four

"I'll pay you back," I say as Julie reluctantly pulls a twenty out of her purse.

She gives me a look.

"I will," I promise, plucking the bill out of her fingers.

"Right," she says. "Miss I-never-have-any-money?"

"Don't worry," I insist. I do have money. It's part of my secret. In fact, I have one thousand nine hundred sixty-one dollars and forty-six cents, now minus twenty bucks. I'm no good at math, but I am good at counting.

I haven't told Julie about the hidden stash in my underwear drawer that I've saved the past two years from allowance, babysitting, and dog walking Mrs.

Testa's poodles. I just promise again to repay her, then hand the twenty dollars over to the girl in the kiosk.

"You're on," I say to Maia. "Are you sure you really, really want pierced ears?"

Maia climbs onto the chair. "Yup."

I don't see any doubt in her eyes. "Okay," I say. "It's going to pinch a little," I lie, just like a nurse. I call this a *lie of kindness.* I don't even want to think what Daddy would call it.

The ear piercer makes little black marks on Maia's lobes. I nod to say the marks are in the right places. The hole puncher is lined up, and pow.

Maia's lower lip trembles, but she doesn't cry. I want to cry for her. Oh boy, did I do the wrong thing? What am I thinking? My poor, poor, poor baby sister. Maybe I should stop—

Pow.

Too late, the other ear is pierced and Maia is sliding off the seat, a huge grin plastered on her face. Her eyes are squinted shut with joy, and only one tear slips out. Small gold balls adorn her lobes.

"They look great," I say.

"You look so old," Julie says. "And so pretty."

"It didn't even hurt," Maia says, wiping a sleeve over her cheek.

I hug her, careful not to squeeze her ears into her head. "You're such a big girl!"

"We have to celebrate," Julie says. She looks at her watch. "Mom's not coming to pick us up for another hour. How about ice cream at O'Malley's?"

Maia beams. "I like ice cream!"

"Me, too," Julie says, taking her hand.

I follow, because I have no choice. Really, I don't mind. I just don't want Sean to think I'm following him around. See, Sean's grandfather started O'Malley's as a small hotdog and ice cream place years ago. Now they have about ten locations all over Connecticut. Not that Sean would be at the mall restaurant this afternoon, but I happen to know that he does go there a lot with his friends for free food.

I'm a little nervous when we enter O'Malley's. The lighting is low and booths line the walls. A salad bar sits off to the right, and to the left is the ice cream bar. We sit on that side of the large room.

After we're seated, I glance around. No sign of Sean or his friends. Sean I like, but Matt and Greg I can do without. Unfortunately, the other two stick to Sean like ticks. I breathe a sigh of relief. Or is it disappointment?

"We're just going to have the ice cream bar," Julie says to the waitress, who then brings us large glass bowls that are more oblong than round.

Maia is first in line. I'm right behind her, holding her bowl. The tradition is that she points and I scoop.

"Well?" I say a few moments later. "What do you want?"

Maia is on her tiptoes, but she still can't really see into the containers.

"This one's Rocky Road, you know, with nuts and marshmallows and chocolate?" I'm sure she'll want some of this. I reach for the scoop.

"What's that?" she says, pointing.

"That's mint chocolate chip, your favorite."
I reach for that scoop. But noooo, she points to another.

"Look, this is butter pecan, this is double chocolate fudge, here is candy apple pie . . ." I move down the line, reading off the names to her. "So?" I say when I'm done. "What do you want?" I notice a small line is forming behind us. "Hurry up."

"What's this one again?" Maia asks.

"Butter pecan. Want some?"

Maia shakes her head. "I want chocolate road."

Finally. I reach for the Rocky Road scoop. I think I hear a long sigh of relief from the line behind me.

"Wait," Maia says. "I want the apple pie."

"You can have both," I say. "In fact you can have five scoops if you really want them. Let's just hurry up and make a decision."

I admit, by this point I'm a little nervous about her pierced ears. After all, I was so sure she was a good ice cream chooser that I figured she was ready to make the pierced-ear decision. Only, this whole ice cream scene isn't going very well. Maybe I should have just bought her plastic clip-on earrings.

At last she makes her choices, and it only takes five minutes to decide what to put on top—whipped cream, nuts, mini M&Ms, crushed candy bars (oh no! five varieties!), caramel sauce, chocolate sauce, strawberry syrup, and a special fall pumpkin sauce. By the time we get back to the table, half the ice cream is melted.

It's my turn to go up and make an ice-cream creation, but I'm so sick of the stuff by now, I just plop in some mint chocolate chip and don't even go for the toppings.

Then, to make matters worse, Sean appears out of nowhere.

"Hi," he says, standing next to our table.

I practically drop my spoon. Quickly I gulp down some water so I don't have to answer him.

Julie kicks me under the table as she says, "Hi, Sean. What are you doing here?"

I look around for his two tick friends. So far so good.

Sean notices me looking and he frowns a little. Then he answers Julie with a grin. "I hear the food is really good here."

I think his grin is a little bigger than it really

needs to be. Does he like Julie? How could he? How couldn't he?

"I like ice cream," Maia announces, banging her spoon into her bowl. Muddy-colored goo splatters onto the table.

"Maia, behave," I warn her, but she just giggles at me.

"Cute," Sean says. "How old are you?"

Maia holds up five sticky fingers.

Sean nods. He looks at me. "Is she your sister?"

Gee, ya think? But I bite my tongue before that slips out. I just nod and guzzle some more water. Julie, across the table, is giving me the stink-eye. Doesn't she understand that dreaming about this moment is a lot different than actually living it? Though the way my heart is pounding, I wonder if I will live through it, or if I'll simply have a coronary and die on the spot. Would Sean come to my funeral?

I snap out of that particular fantasy just in time to hear Julie say, "My mom can give you a ride home."

Sean shoots me a sideways glance. "Uh, that'd be great if you're sure she wouldn't mind. It started raining a little while ago."

"No problem," Julie says, practically laughing. I kick her under the table this time, but it doesn't seem to do any good. "You want to sit with us?"

"Sure," Sean says. "Let me just get something to eat. You guys want anything?"

Like I could eat. I shake my head.

He disappears into the kitchen.

"What are you doing?" I whisper yell at Julie.

"Just being friendly."

"You're doing this on purpose," I accuse.

"What do you mean? I didn't know he was going to be here. I was just being nice offering him a ride home. You want him to get all wet and sick and have to stay home from school with a cold?" She grins.

I kick her again as Sean arrives with a cheeseburger and a basket of onion rings. Julie slides over to give him room. Now he's sitting right across from me. I'd kick her again, only I'm afraid I'd miss and get him instead.

Maia is still plowing through her liquid ice cream, but I can't take another bite. I push my bowl away and watch Sean eat. Man, he even eats cute!

He looks up mid-chew and catches me staring. I never noticed how green his eyes are. I can't seem to look away. But he does. He hastily looks down at his plate again and I see a tinge of red cover his freckled cheeks. He finishes his burger in three more bites, then wipes his mouth on the sleeve of his jacket. I guess he gets free food here, but no free napkins.

"We'd better go outside and wait for my mom," Julie says.

I try to clean Maia up, but she's hopelessly sticky. "Don't touch anything," I warn her as we stand.

Immediately she reaches up to take Sean's hand. He only hesitates a second before taking it, goo and all, and I realize that I'm jealous of my five-year-old sister. They lead the way, Julie walking beside me, digging her elbow into my shoulder every other step.

"How cute is that?" she whispers.

I pretend I don't hear her because it is way cute and I don't want him to hear me gushing. Might give him the wrong impression. Or the right one, and that'd be even worse.

Outside it's raining, so we wait under the overhang. I see the limo first. The long black car pulls up and Frank, the driver, jumps out to open the door for us.

"Damn," Julie says, not quite under her breath.

"Wow," Sean says.

"Don't touch anything," I say to Maia.

"Your mother apologizes for not picking you up," Frank says to Julie. "She's caught up in preparations for tomorrow night." Frank actually speaks with a cute British accent. I always tell Julie he should have been the butler.

We all slide into the limo, and somehow I end up next to Sean. (I'm sure Julie planned that.) We're not exactly squished in there like sardines, but next to *is* next to, even if there is three feet of space between us.

The seats are slippery leather, so when we turn an especially sharp corner, I slide right into him. In my haste to scramble back to my side of the limo, I somehow get my legs tangled with his and we both end up on the floor as Frank hits the brakes for a red light.

While I'm dying of embarrassment, Maia thinks this is a free-for-all. She unbuckles the seatbelt Julie made her wear and jumps on top of us. Frank pulls over to the side of the road and rolls down the privacy glass.

"Is anything wrong back there, Miss Julie?" he asks.

Only Julie can't answer, she's crying too hard. Crying on account of her laughing, the traitor.

I finally manage to scramble back onto the seat, leaving a giggling Maia sprawled across Sean. Sean's face is so red I can't tell where one freckle ends and another one begins.

"Cut it out, Maia," I say, grabbing her arm. She's like a rag doll as I heave her off her new play-mate. I buckle her in again, pulling the seatbelt so tight that she gives me the squinty-eye. Whenever she's mad, she closes her eyes to paper-thin slits and wrinkles her nose. Sometimes it's hard not to laugh. But right now I'm too mortified to even think of laughing.

"We—we're fine," Julie finally gasps out to Frank, who resumes driving, extra slow. Julie's still laughing, and I realize I'll have to kill my best friend.

By this time, Sean is sitting wedged into a corner seat, his feet planted like iron braces, arms crossed defensively over his chest. He really must have hated tangling with me, which hurts my feelings. But even with a broken heart, I can't help thinking about whether it would be totally gross to never again wash my jeans. The jeans that actually came in contact with Sean's jeans.

We drop Sean off first. I knew he lived in this ritzy development, but now I know the exact house. I'm happy to see it's within biking distance from my own house. Not that it even crosses my mind to ride back and forth in front of his driveway on the off chance that he might be sent outside to rake leaves or something, with me just happening to be riding by (maybe for the twentieth time, but he wouldn't need to know that).

His house is really big. Not a mansion like Julie's, but it's all brick and has three garages and lots of points to the roof. I'm glad he doesn't have to see my tiny cottage of a house.

"Thanks for the ride, Jules," he says, using my nickname for her. Who gave him permission to call her that? He opens the door before Frank has a chance to come around and do it for him. "Bye, Maia."

Maia wriggles in her seat like a pleased puppy. "Bye-bye!"

Sean doesn't even look at me. He looks at my knees. Rain's coming in through the open door. "Uh, see ya, slant."

five

"What the—!" Julie starts, but the door slams closed and Sean is running away.

Julie looks at me. Her leftover tears are still there, but the laughing's not. I look away. I don't need any blue-eyed pity.

"Slanty," Maia sings out.

"Stop it!" I nearly shout. I get the squinty-eye, but I don't care and I don't think it's cute anymore. I can't wait to get home to wash my jeans.

The rest of the ride is in silence. I stare out the tinted window at the rain and wind ripping orange leaves from the trees. I try to clear my mind, to forget the cute way Sean ate his burger, or the way he held Maia's hand, the way our legs tangled, him calling me slant. Every time I get to that part, my heart squeezes like a hand holding a baseball.

What did I ever see in him beside freckles, red hair, green eyes, great smile, dimpled cheeks, and big hands? I let his looks blind me, when I should have been looking deeper, then maybe I would have noticed his black heart before he sliced my own in two.

"I don't think he meant to be mean," Julie says as we pull into my driveway.

I look at her, my eyebrows raised. "He called me slant."

"Maybe he thinks you like that name, like it's your nickname or something," Julie says. She throws out her hands palms up when I frown at her. "It's not like you ever tell anyone it bugs you."

It's easy to get out of this argument. I open the door and leave. Maia unbuckles herself and jumps out of the car, landing in a big puddle. The puddle is now all over me. She giggles and races to the house.

Julie shuts the door, but rolls down the window. "You know I'm right." The limo pulls away, the tires crackling over loose gravel. "I'm always right," she calls out.

I ignore her until the limo is out of the driveway, then I turn and stick my tongue out. She leans farther out the window and yells, "I saw that! Real mature, Lauren, real mature!" She waves.

I wave back. I can't help it. She is my best friend, after all. Even if she is annoyingly right sometimes. *Sometimes*, I repeat. *Only sometimes.* Not necessarily *this* time, but *sometimes.* But already I'm having second thoughts about washing my jeans. Maybe I'll just leave them until I know for sure whether Sean is a cute creep or just plain cute.

I'm zapped out of my inner turmoil the minute I step in the front door. Daddy's standing there looking angry and ridiculous at the same time. The ridiculous is on account of his green tights, puffy shorts, puffy shirt, and leather vest. In other words, he looks like a bad version of Robin Hood. And the glasses sitting a bit crooked on his nose don't help. The angry, I see right away, is on account of Maia's ears.

"What were you thinking?" he demands, using his professor voice.

"Nothing," I say. Even I know this is a stupid answer.

"Exactly!" he fumes. "You had no right—absolutely NO right to do this!" He pulls Maia closer and tilts her head so that the little gold balls wink at me. Maia squirms in this uncomfortable position.

"But she wanted them pierced," I say.

"I don't care what she wanted," Daddy says.

"Why shouldn't she have pierced ears?" I ask. "She has the right to make the choice." I take a big breath. "If she's old enough to choose her own ice cream, she's old enough to choose to have her ears pierced." Wow, is that really my argument? Ice cream and ears? What was I thinking? "Isn't she?" I add.

Daddy looks like he can't believe what just came out of my mouth. "Art thou insensible, daughter?" he says, his words starting to sound like his costume.

I shuffle my feet. Maia takes this opportunity to twist out of Daddy's hands and flee to the small television in the living room. Instantly the babble of cartoon voices fills the air.

"You are too young," Daddy says. "You're just a child."

"I'm a teenager. I'm not a baby anymore."

"You're still too young to make decisions like this."

Daddy turns to look at someone who is just walking in from the hall bathroom. "Shelley, you've met my daughter Lauren?"

Shelley steps forward and nods. I recognize her from the college. She's wearing a Maid Marian dress that pretty much matches Daddy's green tights. I wonder if they've planned this. The bodice part of the dress pushes up her breasts so that they look like two pale peaches waiting to be plucked. Her brown hair is piled on her head in impossible swoops and curls, and her blue eyes are wide and round.

"Hello, Lauren," she says, her voice tinkly like crystal glasses tipping together in a toast.

Before I can say hi, Daddy says to her, "What do you think about this mess?"

Shelley shrugs a little. "I wouldn't exactly call it a mess, Martin. Girls get their ears pierced very young nowadays. Even younger than Maia."

Daddy frowns at her.

"But I guess they should have asked first," she adds quickly.

Daddy doesn't look any happier. He jerks open the door and raises a huge, red umbrella. "We're going to a feast," he says shortly. "Watch your sister, and for heaven's sake, don't make any more decisions!" He quickly ushers Shelley out the door, pulling it closed behind him with a loud thunk.

"I'm hungry," Maia calls from the living room.

I pass by her on my way into the kitchen. She's sitting two inches from the TV, not because her eyes don't work, no matter how slanty they are. She just likes being close. Maybe she gets a charge from the static electricity or something.

I start the water boiling for macaroni and cheese, which I've decided we'll have for dinner, feeling pretty sure that this isn't the kind of decision Daddy was talking about not making. Then I run upstairs to change out of my drenched pants. I pull on soft sweats and lay my jeans over the back of my chair to dry. I still haven't decided positively about washing them or not.

After dinner, I sit with Maia and watch a couple shows, then I drag her up to bed. It's not until I'm sitting in my room that I think about Shelley and Daddy. Are they dating? They must be, or why would she be showing off her peachy breasts? Of course, if I had fruit like that, I might want to show them off too. I have cherries at the most.

But is Daddy dating Shelley? Are they kissing? Would he? I can't think much further than that without grossing out. I mean, he's so old! Ugh.

Still, Shelley is pretty. I know she can't be as old as Daddy because last year she was only a gradu-ate student who taught basic English courses at the college. This year Daddy told me she is an adjunct professor. At least she didn't take Daddy's side about the earrings, and I wonder if that's going to hurt their relationship. When Mom was alive, she was the queen, Daddy the jester. The queen made up the rules and took a lot of naps. The jester tried to joke a lot, but you know how lame adult jokes are. After she died, Daddy had to be strong all by himself—no more joking around. I know it was hard on him because he always used to be the softy.

I suddenly miss Daddy's jokes. *What did the banana say to the lettuce? Let's split. What did the lettuce say to the banana? Lettuce leaf now.* Okay, so maybe I don't miss his jokes, but I miss his joking around. His acting silly, making Maia and me giggle, making Mom smile. Sometimes even cracking her up so that her blue eyes squinted nearly shut like mine.

I sigh at the memories. I know they're fading because I can't quite remember the exact blue of Mom's eyes anymore. I know it's a sky blue, but was it an angry, stormy sky, or a clear, summer day sky? I do have photos of her tucked away with my hidden stash of money, but her eyes don't look blue at all in them, they look gray.

I pick up the hand mirror I keep next to my bed. My own eyes are dark brown, almost black. If I pinch the bridge of my nose, the flaps on the inside corners of my eyes pull away so that they're nearly gone. But I can't walk around like that all the time, which is why I wish on every star and pray every night and save every bit of money that comes my way for the operation to have my eyes fixed. I'll never have round eyes, but without the flaps and with a higher eyelid, I'll look more like everyone else, and less like a chinko, or gook (whatever that means), or slant. I won't be told to use toothpicks to keep my eyes open. Like that would even work.

I put the mirror down and roll onto my side. My room is mostly pink and white. I actually have a canopy over my bed. When I was really little, I'd take a nap right here with Mom. We'd cuddle and stare up at the pink bows above us, while Mom told me how she always wanted a canopy bed as a little girl. Then she would fall asleep and I would stay awake, wishing she had always wanted bunk beds instead.

I don't know what's gotten into me, but I get up and pull the canopy off the frame. I've done it before, for the yearly washing, but this time it's not so I can wash the fading pink bows. I tumble the cloth into a bundle and shove it under my bed. The wood and metal frame is more difficult to get rid of. First of all, I'm a bit on the short side. Second, once I finally have everything apart, I don't know what to do with it. The brackets and poles and wires won't fit under my bed. Finally I just lean it all against the back wall of my tiny closet.

I lie down again and stare at the ceiling. I never noticed before that it's all speckled, like someone mixed sand in with the paint. In fact, it even sparkles like body glitter. When I turn off my light, the glow coming in from the hallway gives my ceiling a starlight shimmer, almost as if the Milky Way is splashed above me. This is much more fun than pink bows.

The next thing I know, Daddy is gently shaking me awake. He kisses my brow. He smells like wine and cigarettes, even though he doesn't smoke. After he helps me under the covers, me still in my sweats, he tucks me in till I'm wrapped tight as a mummy.

"You took down your canopy," he whispers.

I pretend I'm asleep. Am I too young to redecorate my room, I wonder. Too young? Too big a decision?

"Pray tell, what am I to do with thee, Lady Lauren?"

six

"He was furious," I say to Julie. We are flopped on her mammoth bed. Her parents are having the fancy-schmancy party tonight and I'm invited. In a little while we'll go downstairs to help get everything ready for the party, not that we're needed. Mrs. Brandt has hired enough caterers and waitresses and coat people and parking attendants to supply a hotel, but it's still fun to help out.

Julie's eyes widen. "Did he ground you or anything?"

"Nah. I can't remember the last time I was grounded." Of course, I can't remember the last time I disobeyed Daddy either. Then again, he never actually said Maia couldn't get her ears pierced, so I wasn't really disobeying a direct order or anything. Yeah, that's called a *lie of convenience.*

Of course, there was a note waiting for me when I woke up this morning. It was propped up against an empty picture frame on my wide windowsill.

> *Dear Lauren, I am so sorry I got angry with you yesterday. It is hard for me to accept the fact that you and Maia are growing up. You're not our little girls any more. What you did was wrong, however. But then again, I do under-stand your motivation. Somehow we'll have to work together on this thing called "teenager."*
> *I love you, Sir Daddy*

As though this is all about me being thirteen. And even in his writing he refers to *our* little girls. I just don't get it. And I don't tell Julie about the note. It's weird that Daddy doesn't just talk to me, but it's weirder still that I've fallen into his habit and I actually write back.

> *Dear Sir Daddy, I'm sorry I had Maia's ears pierced. I understand why you got mad. But it's really not that big a deal, is it? They look so cute on her. And she really did want it done. I won't do it again. Love, Lauren*

I won't do it again because they're already pierced. I wonder if Daddy will catch that.

"You're lucky," Julie says, interrupting my thoughts. "My dad would have killed me. Or at least docked my allowance, and that's worse!"

We both giggle. Thanks to Julie's allowance, we get to go to the movies whenever we want, have our nails done at least once a week, eat sushi when we're in the mood, and even go crazy at the Shoe Emporium every once in a while. And best of all, it lets me save my money, because Julie always insists on paying for everything. Julie doesn't know it, but she's helping make my dream come true.

I sit up, suddenly remembering. "Oh! I forgot to tell you!"

"What?"

"Daddy had a date!"

"What!"

"Yes, a real, live, breathing date! Her name is Shelley and she's pretty pretty and seems nice. She works at the college. I've met her before, but I don't think they were dating then."

"Wow!" Julie still sounds stunned. "Is this the first date since . . ."

"Yeah, since my mom died." I think a minute. "At least I think it's his first one."

Julie looks at me sideways. "How do you feel about it?"

I shrug. "Fine. Why?"

"You don't think of it like your dad's cheating on your mom or anything?"

"Am I the only one who knows my mom is dead?" I say, thinking of how Daddy always says *our* when there is no more *our*. "How can he cheat on a dead woman?"

Julie sticks her tongue out at me. "I didn't mean it like that, and you know it. I just wonder if it feels strange to you. Are you jealous?"

"No way. I'm glad he's dating. Maybe he won't be so weird anymore. Although Shelley *was* wearing clothes from the front of a romance novel." I shrug. "At least he'll have someone to be weird with."

"Maybe she'll be your new mom."

Now that comment makes me feel weird, but I don't say anything. I don't want another mom. I just want Daddy to date and be happy, and to maybe talk like a normal person, stop writing notes, and maybe, just maybe, crack some of his corny jokes again.

I bounce off the bed. "Come on, let's go see what we can do to get in the way and drive your mom crazy."

Julie and I race down the wide, curving front stairs. This mansion has at least four staircases that I know of, and that's not including the one in the secret passage that goes from the first master bedroom suite down to the kitchen.

The first floor is organized chaos. Mrs. Brandt is

whipping around, followed by her personal assistant, shooting orders right and left, tasting food that is being offered to her on silver trays, rearranging perfectly arranged flowers—it looks like a scene from a movie. When she sees Julie, she stops and frowns.

"Why isn't your hair dressed yet?" she asks. Then she looks at me. "Hello, Lauren."

I wave. Mrs. Brandt scares me. If Julie is an oversized fairy, her mother is a life-sized queen who just might say, "Off with her head!" Mr. Brandt, on the other hand, is not a king but a gentle giant. He is nowhere in sight. He knows better.

"Mom, the party isn't for five hours. I don't want to sit around in hair spray for that long. I told Marie to come back at four."

"At four Marie is doing my hair," Mrs. Brandt says, checking the pad of paper her assistant is holding out.

"Then I'll just do my own hair."

"No, Marie will be at your room at three." She looks at me. "Lauren, dear, would you like your hair done up too?"

"Uh, no, that's okay, I—"

Mrs. Brandt nods and walks away, waving for her assistant to follow more closely.

"Argh!" Julie says under her breath.

"You're not a pirate," I say. "Come on, let's go check out the kitchen." I know it's not her favorite room in the house, but she knows how much I love food, so she'll go for my sake. Resisting all the food will at least get her mind off her mother and hair issues. Sometimes I'm glad I'm poor and have pin-straight hair. Sometimes.

The kitchen is amazing. It's about the size of my whole house and yard. It practically blinds me with all its stainless steel and shiny marble—or is it granite? All five ovens look occupied, as do the five huge refrigerators. The Brandts have about four serious parties a year, which are pretty much the only times the kitchen is used. Between parties, they eat out a lot.

All the counters are piled with more food than seems possible, including cut fruit, tiny sandwiches, stuffed olives, little chocolaty things that look amazing, and hundreds of fancy hors d'oeuvres, each held in place with a toothpick. *Toothpicks.*

"What are you doing?" Julie asks as I peel back the plastic wrap from one of the trays.

I pluck a toothpick out of a fat shrimp wrapped in something green and red and balanced on a triangle of black bread. The toothpick is pointy at one end and carved into a miniature design at the other. As far as little slivers of wood go, it is exceptional, but I can't help hearing Matt and Greg telling me to use toothpicks to keep my slanty eyes open. I snap it in half.

Julie is my best friend for so many reasons, but one of them is definitely because she can read my mind. She doesn't say another word, and neither do I. We work silently and stealthily, sidestepping kitchen crew and acting innocent when anyone official passes by. Fifteen minutes later, every toothpick has been removed and thrown away.

After that, we race upstairs, but we don't gloat or giggle. It was a mission and it had to be done. Julie understands that.

The guests start to arrive at seven. We watch from Julie's window at first, then we make our way down to the party. We are the only "children" invited, but everyone knows Julie is the Brandts' daughter and I am her best friend. At least most people know. At the last Fourth of July party a man asked me to take his dirty plate, then another guest whispered something to him and he coughed and walked away from me without even an apology. Whatever.

The best part of the night is when I hear one lady say to Mrs. Brandt, "These canapés are simply delightful. What an unusual twist to make us eat them with our fingers. I always use toothpicks for something like this, but I did read somewhere, maybe it was in Martha Stewart's magazine, that eating with one's fingers is so primal and sensual and really gets us back to our ancestral roots. After all, we were all cave people once." Then she licks the cocktail sauce off her fingers and I think Mrs. Brandt is going to have a coronary. Mrs. Brandt disappears into the kitchen for a few minutes, and the next thing a couple waitresses come out and whisk away the hors d'oeuvres. When they are returned, new toothpicks have been inserted. Oh well. I tried.

Sunday morning I wake up groggy. I didn't get to bed until one in the morning after the party, and peering at my bedside clock, I see that it is now ten. My ears are killing me. If I lie on either side of my head, not only does my earlobe ache, but the sharp back on the earring jabs into my neck, so I have to lie perfectly straight on my back. Are pierced ears really worth all this pain? What a dumb question!

As tired as I am, I'm smiling as I get up and get dressed. Each peek in the mirror assures me that the golden orbs on my ears are definitely worth the agony. After all, I tell myself, I can't be afraid of a little pain. The slicing and stitching of surgery is bound to hurt more than two holes in my ears, and there is no way that I am going to chicken out. There's just the small problem of figuring out how to convince Daddy to give me permission.

I hear clinking and clunking and voices coming up from the kitchen. Odd. Sunday mornings are usually quiet in our house, with Daddy correcting essays and Maia either glued to a PBS station or playing in her room.

As soon as I open my door I realize that it's not just Daddy and Maia causing a racket in the kitchen—someone else is in there with them. A woman's voice laughs and says, "Keep stirring, keep stirring!"

When I make it to the kitchen, everyone glances at me, smiles, and then continues on with what they are doing. Daddy is cooking up something that smells like bacon in the microwave and toasting English muffins in the toaster. Maia, standing on a chair, is stirring something with a whisk over the stove while Maid Marian (aka Shelley) keeps one arm around Maia's waist and one hand on the pot handle.

"Keep stirring, honey," Shelley says. "You're doing a great job."

"Eggs Benedict," Daddy says as a greeting.

"Hope you like them," Shelley says.

"I'm making the holiday sauce," Maia says, not taking her eyes off the pot.

"It's hollandaise sauce," I say. "And I love eggs Benedict."

Shelley grins at me. "You know the secret to the best hollandaise sauce?"

"More than enough lemon," I say. I should know, it's practically my favorite dish in the world. Definitely my favorite brunch food.

"You're brilliant," Shelley says with a laugh, and squeezes another half a lemon into the sauce.

"Wouldst thou squeeze us some juice of orange?" Daddy asks, juggling toasted muffins and a plate of steaming ham slices.

Happy to help out, I cut up the bag of oranges by the sink and press each one in the juicer we got for Christmas last year and only used once. I'm wondering what the special occasion is when I catch Shelley and Daddy glancing at each other and smiling. Oh. It's actually pretty cute to see the crush they have on each other. Shelley is obviously the special occasion, and I could certainly get used to eggs Benedict every weekend, so I have no problem with this.

We finally sit down to eat. It feels a little weird to have four of us around the kitchen table, but other than shifting the chairs a bit, no one makes a big deal of it. Shelley dishes up the food and presents it to each of us with a "Ta-da!" The egg yolks are perfectly runny, the sauce has just the right tang to it, the muffins aren't burnt, and the ham is sweet.

"Totally yummy," I say with my mouth full. It is the best eggs Benedict I've ever had.

"I made the holiday sauce," Maia says, her eyes all squinty with joy.

Daddy just nods and smiles and chews.

Beaming, Shelley looks around the table,

catches my eye and winks, then digs in. There's not much talking as we devour our food. Luckily we're all fast eaters and we finish up around the same time. There are no seconds, but no one seems hungry for more.

Daddy pats his stomach, does one last swipe at his mouth with his napkin, then lays it aside. "Whew! What a meal!"

"If I keep eating like this," Shelley says, patting her stomach, "I won't fit into the dress for the fair next weekend."

"What fair?" I ask.

"It's a medieval fair on Saturday," Shelley says. "Have you ever been to one?"

I shake my head.

"Oh, they are so much fun. You should come with us. You and Maia would have a wonderful time. There are games, and interesting food, and lots to see. Everyone dresses up in medieval clothing."

"We don't have anything to wear," I say.

Shelley waves her hand. "No problem. I have old dresses we can cut down to fit you. Come on, it'll be fun!"

"You don't have to," Daddy says, but he looks hopeful.

I know he goes to fairs and parties like this, but he's never asked us to come along. I look at Maia. She's whisking the leftover hollandaise sauce on her plate with her fork.

"Okay," I say. "Sounds like fun." Anyway, I know Julie will be gone on Saturday. Her mom and aunt are taking her to a spa in Norwich for the day. Julie says she hates to go, but I think she just says that so I don't feel bad about not being invited. Like I would want to spend the day with her scary mother and her even scarier aunt. Don't think so.

"That's great," Shelley says.

"Such joy, such joy you doth bring to mine heart," Daddy says. Why he can't just say, "Glad to hear it," I don't know.

Shelley doesn't seem to mind though. She reaches over and squeezes his hand and they smile into each other's eyes.

"So what time do we pick up Grandma?" I say. As soon as the words are out of my mouth, I realize that's a low blow. Daddy looks suddenly tired, the glow gone from his eyes.

He glances at his watch. "Her plane lands at one, so we should probably clean up and get going in an hour or so."

Shelley jumps to her feet. "Right. And I've got some research to do at the library, but I'll help do the dishes first."

"No, no, that's okay," Daddy says, ushering her out of the kitchen. I hear the murmur of their voices in the tiny foyer.

I clank the dishes loudly so they don't think I'm trying to eavesdrop. We don't have a dishwasher—

or rather, I should say that the dishwasher's name is Lauren—so I'm a little bummed that Daddy isn't letting Shelley stay to help. In fact, I'm wondering why he's rushing her out of here.

Shelley pops her head through the door. "Bye, girls. I'll be in touch about those dresses."

Maia rushes over to her and hugs her around the hips. Shelley laughs and hugs her back. I wave from the sink with soapy hands, glad to have an excuse to skip the hug. After all, I barely know her. It's like kissing—first date or second or third? As if I have to worry about that! I plunge my hands back into the hot water and try not to think about Daddy and Shelley and their first kiss. First date? Second? Third? Ick!

seven

It's not that Daddy is late for everything. In fact, he usually starts off way ahead of time. But he always forgets something and has to turn around to retrieve it. Sometimes that even happens more than once.

In this case, we leave plenty early to reach Bradley International Airport in time, but then Daddy realizes he forgot what airline she is flying in on, so we have to return to get that information, only he'd written it on a tiny slip of paper that was a cinch to get lost in his messy office. It takes us fifteen minutes to find it. Maia is not a help, by the way. Many of Daddy's essays now need to be repaginated. Luckily he tells all his students to label and number every page because he has a young daughter who likes to play throw-the-papers-around when no one is looking.

The second time we have to go back to the house because Daddy remembers that he forgot his wallet, and knowing his luck he'll be pulled over with Grandma Ann in the car and she'll cluck her tongue at him. I'm surprised to actually hear him say all this out loud.

I don't remember Grandma Ann as a tongue clucker. I remember her as a large, squishy lady in dark clothing. When Mom was alive, Grandma Ann and Grandpa Joe flew up from Florida at least once a year for a weeklong visit. Mom took lots of naps when they visited. Then Grandpa Joe died and we all flew down to Florida for the funeral. I barely remember Grandpa Joe or his funeral, but I do remember the side trip to Disney World and Peter Pan's ride. In fact, Grandma Ann looks a lot like a softer version of Captain Hook— big nose, dyed black hair and all. No hook hand though.

After Grandpa Joe died, Grandma Ann came up to visit twice a year. I don't know why Mom always got extra tired when Grandma was around, but she took even longer naps during these visits.

Finally we are on the road for real. We make it to the airport just as Grandma Ann's plane is expected to land. With all the new rules and regulations, we can't wait for her at her gate, so we park the car in short-term parking and wait at the baggage claim area.

I see her first. She's wearing a bright orange jogging outfit and sneakers. She carries an old-fashioned, Nanook-of-the-North type winter coat over one arm and a huge purse/duffel bag over the other.

Besides the neon-colored outfit, the most surprising thing is her hair. It's white. We always knew she dyed it black because she said it made her feel younger. Now it is her natural color, and I actually think she looks younger. Or maybe it's because she doesn't look like she's dressed for a funeral.

She gives me a tight hug. "Oh, darling, you're so grown up!" she says. "You are a young lady! A teenager! My goodness!" Then she sees Maia, who is suddenly shy and hiding behind Daddy's legs. Grandma crouches down. "And who is this? Why, you were a wee baby last time I saw you! Come hug your Grandma Ann, little one."

Maia sidles up to her and gives her a half hug. Grandma lifts her up in her big arms. Maia giggles.

"Hello, Ann," Daddy says. He gives her a slight smile as he fiddles with the ear piece on his glasses.

"Martin, so good to see you. Thank you so much for having me." She hugs him with her coat arm. The purse arm is still holding up Maia. "I simply

couldn't miss Miss Lauren's thirteenth birthday!"
She smiles mistily at me.

We retrieve her luggage: two large zebra-print
suitcases . . . for one week? I can't help wondering if I misread her card and she's really staying
for a month. I see Daddy eyeing them and probably wondering the same thing. Daddy and I drag
it all out to the car. Maia is in her element because
the nice, giant lady is still carrying her. And while
Daddy has remembered his wallet, he's forgotten
to put any money in it, so Grandma Ann has to pay
for parking, and sure enough, I hear her cluck her
tongue. Poor Daddy's ears turn red.

We make it home in about forty minutes.
Grandma Ann talks the whole time. I know that
her hair is now white because her age is nothing
to be ashamed of, though she doesn't actually say
her age. She has three boyfriends in Florida, but
she thinks one is cheating on her. She is the bingo
champion of Evergreen Meadows Lot C and has
won nearly one thousand dollars—but don't tell
anyone because she's really not sure if she's supposed to pay taxes on it or not. She may have
to have cataract surgery in the next year. She is
learning tai chi and Reiki and meditation. She has
converted to Buddhism, though once in awhile
she still goes to Catholic mass to see her friends.
I am exhausted by the time we get home, and I
wonder if that's why Mom took so many naps.

Daddy runs up to his office to clean the mess we made looking for the flight information. He'd pretty much forgotten he needed to clean it for Grandma's visit anyway, so he promises to do that now. Maia goes to her room to play with her dolls. So I'm stuck with Grandma Ann. Stuck is not the nicest word, but after the party last night and the big brunch, I wouldn't have minded just chilling on my bed and reading or going over to Julie's house to watch a movie in their home theater. But I can't very well leave Grandma alone in the living room after she's flown up here to see me for my birthday, so I sit with her.

As soon as we're settled with a root beer for me and tea for Grandma, she rattles on some more about what she's been doing for the last three years in Florida. I'm beginning to think this is going to be a very, very long afternoon, when she mentions my present.

"I've been wanting to give this to you for some time now," Grandma says, leaning forward and placing a hand on my knee.

I smile expectantly. "Okay."

For some reason tears fill her eyes. Uh-oh. This isn't how a present giving is supposed to go, is it?

Grandma Ann blinks rapidly and reaches for one of her suitcases. Laying it flat on the floor, she unzips it and removes a large box, which she hands to me.

It's heavy. It's not wrapped. It looks like a large gift box that you might put a sweater in from Saks or somewhere, only it's white. It's not even taped closed, so I easily lift off the lid. Inside is a photo album, tucked neatly into the center of the box and held in place with scrunched-up tissue paper.

"Go ahead, open it," Grandma says. I hear a sniffle in her voice.

I raise the cover. A young girl looks at me, smiling shyly. I know her. She looks familiar, but not.

"It's your mother," Grandma whispers. "These are pictures of sweet Charlene."

Wow, I think. Then I have to say it. "Wow. Mom?" I turn a page. The photos are old-fashioned looking, not the glossy prints I get from my digital camera at CVS. Some even have white borders. They are stuck behind waxy sheets of clear plastic to keep them in place. Some of the photos are permanently stuck in place and would be ruined if I tried to remove them.

Mom in a kiddie pool, Mom in the bathtub, Mom in a Brownie uniform, Mom at Christmas next to the tree, Mom with braces, Mom without braces—Grandma explains each photo in detail. It takes us a long time to get toward the end, but I don't mind. I realize how much I don't know about my own mother. Sure, she died when I was almost ten, but even when she was alive she didn't talk much about her childhood, and since she's been gone, Daddy hardly says a word about her, and Grandma Ann hasn't been up to visit.

Mom has short blonde hair in most of the pictures, and she smiles a lot, but something doesn't look quite right.

I turn the page, nearly at the end of the album, and gasp. It's the nose.

"It's the nose," Grandma says as though she can read my mind like Julie always does. "She had a deviated septum that needed to be fixed, so the doctor offered to do a reduction at the same time."

"What's a deviated septum?" I ask, when I really just want to ask about the "reduction."

"It's when the nasal passage up here goes too much to one side or the other." She points to the bridge of her nose. "It's a simple procedure to correct it. Charlene was having breathing difficulties because of it." She shrugs. "And she always hated her nose, so she had a reduction performed as well."

"Wow," I can't help saying again. "How old was she?"

"Thirteen."

A tingle buzzes through me. My mom had corrective surgery (I've done my homework and I know that's what it's called) at *my* age. The change is amazing. Not that I noticed that she had a huge nose in the earlier photos—in fact, I couldn't even tell what was off, just that she didn't look quite how I remembered her. But now that I see the after shot, I am amazed how much prettier she is with a cute, snubby nose. The last three pages are full of Mom post–nose operation. She is beautiful. And Grandma let her have the operation. At thirteen!

I close the album.

"Do you like the present?"

"I love it," I say, and I mean it.

"I could have gotten you a gift certificate or something—"

"No way," I interrupt. "This is great." I hug the album to my chest. "Thank you so much."

Grandma Ann's almost-need-cataract-surgery blue eyes tear up again. "I'm so glad you like it. Your mother would be so proud of you now. You're growing up to be such a lovely young lady." She leans over and hugs me. I let her.

She lets go and I say tentatively, "Grandma . . ." Do I dare ask her? "I need a—a huge favor."

"Anything, Lauren. I'd do anything for you. And I'm so sorry I've stayed away for so long, but I promise I won't stay away any longer. I'll do anything for you, dear."

I take a big breath. Promising to do anything and actually doing this might be two different things. "I want an eye operation and I need you to come to the doctor with me," I blurt out.

"Oh no," she exclaims with a slight laugh. "You're too young to have cataracts!" She pauses. "Aren't you? Why, I've never heard of such a thing."

"I don't have cataracts, Grandma," I say. "I want this flap removed to make my eyes less—less slanty."

"But you have very pretty eyes!"

"No I don't. I have *chink* eyes. Boys tell me to use toothpicks to keep them open. I hate them!" Have I actually ever said these words out loud? I feel horrified and thrilled at the same time. "They call me gook, and chink, and—and slant. If I have the operation, I'll have round eyes. I'll have eyelids more than I have now. I won't be teased. Please, Grandma!" My throat feels tight and my hands are clenched into fists. Even though I've thought and wished and prayed about this for so long, they were always silent words—words on the inside. Somehow, putting it all out there feels like needles jabbing my heart.

Grandma Ann looks a little shocked, and I'm not sure if it's sadness or cataracts fogging her eyes. "Have you talked to your father about this?"

I shake my head. "He won't understand. I couldn't even get my ears pierced until I turned thirteen. He'll never agree. But I've saved all the money. They're my eyes. Please?"

Grandma looks at me for a long moment. She

reaches out and strokes my hair. "Okay, Lauren, if that's what you truly want, I'll take you to the plastic surgeon's office, at least for a consultation. I want you to be happy. No one deserves to be unhappy."

I leap up and hug her. My arms don't even connect around her broad shoulders. "Thank you so much, Grandma. This operation will make me the happiest girl in the world, I promise!" And I believe it with all my soul.

eight

"Are you going to the Fall Frolic?" Julie asks me. It's Monday and we are standing in the cafeteria, about to get in line. It's fish patties or ham sandwiches, so no one is rushing to eat. People are lining up at the ticket table to buy tickets to the dance.

"I doubt it," I say. "Are you?"

"I was thinking about asking Danny Sidowicz," Julie says.

"What?" I grab her arm and turn her to face me. "Danny? The one who snorts when he laughs?"

"It's cute when he does that," Julie says, blushing. "He sits next to me in French and helps me out."

I shake my head. "He barely comes up to your shoulder."

"I like short guys," she says.

"Like you have a choice. You're the tallest one in this school." I think she's even taller than most of the teachers, but I don't say that out loud.

"Why don't you ask Sean?" Julie says, ignoring my last comment.

"No way." It's my turn to blush.

"I think he likes you."

"Yeah, that's why he called me *slant*?" I still haven't washed my jeans, just in case.

"I told you, he probably thinks you like that nickname."

"Okay, whatever." That's what I say when I want to end a conversation. But Julie knows me too well.

"It's not like you've ever told anyone to shut up about it." Sometimes Julie is like a dog with a juicy bone.

"Nice weather we're having," I say.

"You're just too chicken. You have to speak up for yourself, you know, Lauren."

"Did you hear that the Jersey Devils won another game?"

"*I* told *you* about the Devils, like you care about hockey, and you're only changing the topic because you know I'm right, and I'm only letting you change the topic because I know you know I'm right." With that she gets in line so she can pick through the salad bar and hardly eat any of it anyway.

"Whatever," I grumble behind her. I have to get in the last word even if she doesn't hear me.

Everyone is talking about the Fall Frolic. For three days in a row, I linger at the end of math, wondering if Sean will wave to me or wave to Mr. Driggs and I can just pretend he is waving to me. But he hasn't waved to either of us by Wednesday. The dance is less than two weeks away and I: a) can't get Sean's attention, and b) can't get up the nerve to ask him to the dance. Either way it looks like I'll be sitting home alone that Friday night, especially if my soon-to-be ex–best friend asks Danny out. But no wonder she has guts—she's tall, blonde, and beautiful. I'd be braver too, if I looked like Julie. I may as well face it, no one wants to go to a dance with someone nicknamed *slant*.

"For homework," Mr. Driggs's voice drones on, "finish the even-numbered problems on page seventy-five."

I flip to the back of the textbook. There are over four hundred pages! Math is going to drag on and on this year.

The bell is about to ring, so half the class clusters together at the door. I take my time putting away my book.

"Hey."

Startled, I look up. "Oh, hi, Sean." He is sooooo cute.

"I haven't seen you at the mall."

"The mall?"

"You know, I saw you there last Friday. I thought maybe you hung out there or something."

I will now. "Sometimes," I say. I shove my book into my bag. I'm willing to risk bruises if it means walking out with Sean.

"Do you like to dance?" he asks.

My heart literally stops beating. Okay, so maybe it doesn't exactly stop, or I'd crash dead to the floor, but it definitely pauses. *This is it! This is it!* "Sure, I love to dance," I say as calmly as possible.

Sean shuffles his feet and glances at me, then at the clock, then at the door. Is he waiting for me to say something? Waiting for the bell to ring so he can escape?

"You?" I say.

"Hunh?"

Now I'm confused too. What were we talking about? Oh, yeah. "Do you like to dance?"

"It's okay. I just wanted to know—"

The bell rings, interrupting him. He shrugs. "Maybe I'll see you at the mall?"

"Sure," I say. I want to grab his arm and demand to know what he was going to say, but of course I don't.

He catches up to Matt and Greg and they look back at me. Matt puts his fingers to the outside corners of his eyes and pulls them into slits and he and Greg laugh. Sean doesn't laugh, but he doesn't tell them to shut up either.

I'm depressed for the next two periods. What was he going to say? Was he going to ask me to the dance? Does he really want to see me at the mall? If I do see him at the mall, what will I say to him?

Even Julie can't snap me out of it during photography.

"At least he talked to you," she says. "That's a good thing."

"I guess," I say.

"If this is what being a teenager does to you," she continues, "I may have to ignore you till you turn twenty." She thinks this is going to make me smile, or at least get me to hit her for threatening not to be my best friend anymore, but she's wrong. I continue to mope.

"I have some news," she says. I hear a strange fizz in her voice. My ears perk up warily.

"What news?" I'm not sure I really want to hear this.

"I asked Danny to the dance during French."

I whirl on her. "You did?"

She nods.

"And?"

"He said yes, of course."

"Of course," I say. I wish I could be as self-assured as Julie. I hate the little gurgle of jealousy I feel in my stomach, and right away I squash it. She's my best friend. She can't help it if she's model beautiful and guys fall at her feet drooling. Well, I've never actually seen a guy do that, but I bet they would if they thought it'd impress her. No one will ever fall at my feet unless I trip him, though that might not be a bad idea the next time Sean walks by.

But I don't see him for the rest of the day. When I get home, Grandma Ann is watching some soap opera in the living room. I'm surprised to see Shelley sitting next to her until I remember that she is coming over today to work on my dress for the medieval fair this Saturday. Yesterday she came by with a dress for Maia. Maia really did look like a princess in the maroon velvet with the pink lace peeking out here and there.

Shelley jumps up as soon as she sees me. "You're home!"

"Hi," I say. I give Grandma Ann a hug.

"Hello, dear." She tries to look at me and the television at the same time. "So you're working on a project with Shelley. How nice." I'm surprised to hear a hint of jealousy in Grandma's voice.

"Do you want to help us?"

"No, no, I'll just watch my show. You two have fun together."

Shelley shrugs at me and we head up to my bedroom to work since I have to try the dress on to be fitted.

"I did ask if she wanted to join us," Shelley says in an undertone.

"It's okay," I say, wondering if it is. Does Grandma have a problem with the woman who is dating her son-in-law?

In my room, Shelley pulls mounds of green material out of a large, white plastic bag. When she shakes it out, I see that it is a shiny green dress that doesn't look nearly as horrid as it sounds. Black ribbon laces up over the chest, and white fringe hangs from the dangly sleeves. I'm sure it looks better lying across the bed than it will on me.

"I won't fit into that," I say bluntly.

Shelley whips out a sewing kit. "That's why I've come prepared. With a little tucking here and there, and some hemming, it'll look like it was made for you. And the green with the black trim will look gorgeous with your black hair and your skin color."

Any fool can see that the dress is beautiful, but that same fool would be able to see that it will take a lot more than some simple "tucking here and there" to get the dress to fit. But, keeping my bare back to Shelley, I slip it over my head at her urging. What choice do I have?

As I expected, the dress puddles on the floor—way too long for me. And the waist is too wide, never mind the bust area. It'd take a whole box of Kleenex to fill it properly.

Shelley turns me toward the full-length mirror on the back of my door. "Okay," she mumbles with pins in her mouth. "This'll be easy." She pulls the dress tight in the back. I don't even look in the mirror. I'm trying to figure out a way to get out of making a complete idiot of myself at the fair in this giant dress. I'll pretend I'm sick or I have a last-minute essay to write. No way can I go out in public like this.

A few minutes later, Shelley says, "Okay, that's it."

I whirl gratefully away from the mirror without even a peek.

"Don't you want to see what it'll look like after the alterations?"

I shake my head.

Shelley shrugs. "Do you have any homework? I could work on this downstairs if you do."

I think of Grandma giving Shelley the stink-eye during the commercials. "No, you can stay up here. I can do my work later." I watch her thread a needle with green thread, double it over, and knot it at the end. "I'll help you sew if you want," I offer. "I took sewing for a quarter last year." I don't bother telling her I only got a C+ in the class. Who knew sewing a straight line on a machine would be so hard? Mrs. Anderson had said it was a good thing I wasn't driving yet—the way I hit the sewing pedal I'd be going ninety miles an hour on the road. Besides, sewing by hand has to be easier, right?

"That would be great," Shelley says, beaming at me. She hands me the threaded needle and shows me where to start hemming.

We work in silence for a little while. The agonized voices from the soap opera downstairs make a dull background noise.

"So, what's your favorite subject in school?" Shelley asks.

"Math," I say without thinking. *Math?* My face heats up immediately and I hope Shelley can't see my blush. "I mean English."

Shelley chuckles. "Both? Most people like one or the other. Me, I was terrible in math, but I could diagram a sentence with my eyes closed."

"English," I say firmly. I just like math because of Sean. What a dummy! "Definitely English."

"Just like your dad," Shelley says.

Yeah, I think, *just like my* adopted *dad.* I wonder if Shelley maybe wasn't so good in science in school either. She does understand that genetically I didn't get my love of English class from my father, right? But I'm too polite to ask.

"Your dad's really brilliant, you know."

Actually, I didn't know. Who thinks of their dad as brilliant? Or even datable, for that matter.

She continues with, "And he says the same about you. '*My* brilliant Lauren,' he calls you."

"Really?" I say. "He says '*my* brilliant Lauren'?"

Shelley nods, glancing up at me inquisitively.

Hmm, I wonder. Maybe this dating is doing a lot more than I thought.

"What does he call Maia?"

Shelley grins. "*My* little, mischievous Maia."

"That's so true," I say, laughing. Shelley laughs with me, and a funny little warmth glows in my stomach. I look up at her through my bangs. I like the way the sides of her eyes crinkle when she laughs. I don't remember Mom's eyes crinkling like that. I remember her putting a lot of lotion on her face to keep the wrinkles away.

A few minutes later, I say, "Um, thank you for helping me with the whole pierced-ear thing. Daddy was really upset."

"Martin, I mean your dad, told me later I shouldn't have interceded."

"Oh, sorry. Was he mad at you?"

"He got over it. I think he thought we were ganging up on him. For all his brilliance, he doesn't really understand women. Especially after what happened with your mom . . . he somehow feels like he failed."

The warm glow in my stomach is gone. Instead, I feel a bit of a fist in there. "It wasn't his fault she fell and hit her head," I say.

Shelley's fingers pause, and she glances at me before resuming her sewing. "No, of course not," she agrees, bending lower over her stitches as though she can't see them clearly. "None of it was his fault."

I don't understand the tension in the air. Downstairs, the soap operas must be over because wild cheering jars my nerves. Must be *Oprah* time.

"I'm sorry I brought up your mom," Shelley says quietly.

More cheering.

"It's okay," I say with a shrug. "I guess I'm just not used to it. Daddy never ever talks about her. But Grandma Ann just gave me this." I set aside my sewing and bounce off the bed. When I return I'm holding the photo album. "Want to see?"

"Sure." Shelley moves aside the piles of fabric to make room on her lap for the album. Slowly she flips through the pages. I don't say anything until near the end.

"This is her after her nose job," I finally say.

Shelley turns back a page or two to see the difference. "She really didn't need it, did she? She was beautiful."

"But she wasn't happy before," I explain.

"Oh, I see."

I look closely at the photos after her operation as Shelley examines the last few pages. I look for that spark of happiness my mother must have felt at finally having the nose she'd always wanted. Shelley closes the album and hands it back to me.

"Thanks for sharing that with me, Lauren. I really appreciate it." She picks up her sewing. "Have you shown it to your dad?"

I start sewing again too. "Not yet," I say. What I don't say is that I probably never will.

"Oh." We sew in silence. Then, "Maybe you could put some of the pictures in those empty frames you have there."

I look over at my windowsill. I have at least ten blank frames staring at me. Some are plain wood or metal, and some are decorated with flowers or animals. My favorite frame I found in our basement when I was exploring last year. It's very old and carved with vines and hidden faces. The whole thing is covered in gold. Daddy says it's real gold.

"I guess I could," I finally say.

"Why don't you have any pictures in them?" she asks.

I shrug, but she doesn't see me because she's inspecting her stitches. "I just haven't had the time," I lie. This is a *lie of stupidity*. I mean, how long can it possibly take to put a photo in a frame? But Shelley doesn't call me on it. I used to have pictures in frames all over my room. But pictures don't keep mommies alive.

—

An hour later, the tips of my fingers feel like pincushions. Hopefully Shelley won't notice the two dots of blood I've left on the underside of the hem.

"I think that's it," Shelley says at last, shaking out the dress. "It should fit you like a gorgeous, jeweled glove now."

I eye it dubiously. It still looks too big for me, especially in the chest area.

"Come on, you have to try it on," Shelley says.

I can see that I don't have a choice. Keeping my back to her and to the mirror, I let Shelley help me slip it over my head. Then she laces up the front and back until I am no longer swimming in the fabric and it fits tight around my waist and even my chest.

Shelley steps back and claps her hands. "Oh. My. God."

"What's wrong?" I say, startled by her reaction.

"Absolutely nothing." She firmly grabs my shoulders and turns me toward the mirror.

I nearly faint. Is that really me in the mirror? I have this tiny waist, and the skirt flares out from there and just touches the ground enough to crinkle a little when I walk. But it's the top part of the dress that I can't believe. The puffy shoulders, the lace at the wrists . . . the boobs!

I'm speechless. Julie would have called 9-1-1 by now, thinking I was choking on something or someone had cut out my voice box.

Shelley steps up behind me and peers into the mirror over my shoulder. "Well? Do you like it?"

"I—I can't believe it," I gasp. "I—look!" Words fail me. I point to my chest.

Shelley laughs. "What do you expect? You're thirteen, silly, of course you're growing breasts."

"But I don't even have a bra! I didn't think I needed one."

"Oh, you definitely need one." Shelley is still laughing, but not in a mean way.

The warm glow in my stomach is back. I turn, admiring myself from all angles. Shelley was right. The green dress with the black trim looks wonderful on me with my long, black hair swishing out around my shoulders as I twirl. But no matter how great everything looks as a whole, I can't help staring at my chest. I must have grown them overnight. Or maybe I had been so convinced I'd never have a chest, I just ignored that area for so long, and . . .

"I really do need a bra," I say, giggling. I hate gigglers, but I can't help myself.

"I'll take you to the mall to get one, if you want," Shelley offers.

I'm about to agree, but then I remember Grandma Ann. "I think I'll have Grandma take me," I say. "I mean—"

"No, no, I completely understand," Shelley says quickly. She starts to pack up the sewing kit.

I hope I haven't hurt her feelings, but I think Grandma will be crushed if I don't ask her. I smile to myself. Here I am with two women in my life, when for so long I only had Daddy. I cringe to think of what I would have done if I had to go bra shopping with him! I'd have broken down and asked Mrs. Brandt, the ice queen, before asking Daddy. I shudder at the thought.

I make one more twirl in front of the mirror. This dress would be waaayyy over the top to wear to the Fall Frolic, not that I have a date anyway. But I sure would love Sean to see me in it. For once I feel beautiful and the only people who are going to see me are my family and a bunch of weirdos who dress up in medieval clothes and pretend they're living in the Middle Ages. Just great.

nine

Thursday morning Daddy is already gone with Maia, and Grandma is still asleep. With Grandma sleeping in Daddy's office, I notice that he leaves earlier and comes back later.

He's left me a note next to my cereal bowl though.

> *Dear Lauren,*
> *Thank you so much for being so sweet to Shelley. She complimented me on having such a lovely and brilliant young lady for a daughter. I could tell your kindness made her feel comfortable with you, and I really appreciate it. You are a shining star in my life. I can't wait to see you in your gown, Lady Lauren!*
> *Your loving Sir Daddy*

I smile. I get out a pen, about to write a note in return. But then I stop myself. Is this the only way we know how to "speak" to each other? For some reason this makes me very sad. I don't write back.

The day is uneventful. I work hard to avoid Tweedledum and Tweedledummer (aka Matt and Greg). And Sean seems to be doing a good job of avoiding me. I'm hoping he'll linger at my desk after math like he did yesterday, but he's first in line to be out of the door. So I'm especially depressed when it's time for photography lab.

It's my turn to develop film. The final critique session for the quarter is next week. I can't believe the end of the quarter is looming so close.

I like the darkroom cubicle. While I don't think I'm that great of a photographer, I'm actually rather brilliant, as Daddy might say, at the technical aspects. I can thread the film into the developing canister in the dark, no problemo. I develop the film, stop it, print a contact sheet, and even in the dull glow of the red bulb, I'm pretty impressed with the tiny images that are appearing as if by magic on the photo paper. When it's fully processed, I hang it up to dry.

I flip on the light. I am no Dorothea Lange, that's for sure, but I can't help being impressed by Julie's perfect face. But as beautiful as Julie looks, I can clearly see that the photos are lacking the *glimmer of her soul,* as Miss Shepard would say.

Still, I have to have something for the critique coming up, so I choose five shots to enlarge, then I shut off the overhead bulb again and work under the red light. I experiment a little with over- and underexposing, dodging and burning, until I'm satisfied with three of the five images. Maybe Miss Shepard will be so impressed with how beautiful Julie looks, she won't notice how flat and boring the pictures really are.

I have one last photo to develop. It's the shot I took of Sean leaving the gym. Miraculously, it is in perfect focus. Unfortunately, it's just his back. But I have to say, as far as backs go, his is perfect. I make a small print of it to keep in my English folder, so I can dream over it when I'm doing my homework.

When I get home with Maia, I call out, "Hi, Grandma." The soaps are on in the living room, but Grandma Ann is not lounging on the couch as usual.

Maia heads up to her room as I push into the kitchen through the swinging door and I feel like I've hit a brick wall full in the face. The room is so thick with heaviness I can barely breathe. Grandma is sitting alone at the round, wooden table, a hand-kerchief clutched in her hand, eye makeup not looking too pretty.

I rush over to her. "Grandma, what's wrong?"

She pulls me into her arms and buries her face in my neck. "Oh, baby, baby," she moans. "What did I do wrong? What did I do wrong? I'm so sorry."

I'm scared now. I try to pull out of her hug, but she's about five times bigger than I am. "Grandma, stop it! You didn't do anything wrong!"

Snuffling now, Grandma lets me go, rubbing the handkerchief across her nose and eyes. "This is where it happened. This is where she died. My baby. Ohhhh," she wails. "What did I do wrong?" She reaches for me.

I step back. I can't be caught in those arms again. They might suffocate me.

"It was an accident," I say. My voice is little, even in my own ears. Little and young and scared. My stomach churns. "She fell. She hit her head. Daddy found her. It wasn't your fault. It wasn't anyone's fault. It was an accident." I say it almost like I heard it once so long ago. But it was Daddy talking then. *She fell. She hit her head. I found her. It wasn't your fault. It was an accident.*

I try to believe my words, just like I tried when Daddy said them to me right after my mother died. It was the truth. It is the truth, I say to myself, because Daddy doesn't lie.

Grandma puts her head on her arms on the table, and I leave her there. I stay in my room even after I hear her go back to the living room and flip through the channels, even after I hear Daddy come home, even after Grandma calls me down for dinner. And when Daddy comes up to check on me, I pretend to be asleep. I'm afraid he'll ask me about my day. And while I'd love to tell him about my success in the photo lab, I can't say anything about Grandma's breakdown in the kitchen because then I'd have to ask my own questions, demand real answers. So I simply close my eyes and breathe deeply as he strokes my hair. *Lying by sleeping.* It always works.

—

I wake up Friday morning with a smile on my face. Today is the day! Today I go to see Dr. Sung about my double eyelid surgery.

My stomach growls like a starving lion, and I remember that I "slept" through dinner last night. The house is quiet with Daddy and Maia gone, as usual, and Grandma Ann in her room, though I think I do hear her shuffling around in there with some weird fluty-type music going on. Yoga time maybe?

I'm so hungry I ignore the cereal bowl and head right for last night's leftover chicken parm. Yummy! Even cold I can gobble it down. Part of eating fast is because I'm so hungry, but I know the other part is because I want to be out of the house before Grandma finishes her yoga and finds me in the kitchen.

Eating over the sink, I look at the kitchen table. I've known all along that that was where my mother died, but it never freaked me out. Did Grandma Ann think of it every time she stepped in here? Did Daddy? He was the one who found her. He never even changed the table and chairs after her accident. I try to feel any presence of my mother's spirit, but all I feel is a cold lump of chicken, cheese, and tomato sauce glugging down my throat. I wash it down with a chug of OJ.

It's not that I don't feel bad about my mother's death, and it's not that I don't miss her sometimes even though I was ten when she died. It's just that I've moved on. I feel like Daddy finally is too, now that he's actually dating someone. But Grandma Ann . . . poor Grandma. Maybe she should have come up here to visit us earlier, because even though she doesn't dress like she's going to a funeral anymore, there's still something very dark and bleak about her. I wonder if Dorothea Lange would have been able to capture it in a photo. I wonder if I could, or if I'd even want to.

Everyone loves a Friday. Even the teachers smile more. The only teacher who seems depressed no matter what day it is is Mr. Driggs. But who can blame him? He teaches math, after all.

"Do you want to go to the mall after school?" Julie asks me as I'm sucking down a chocolate pudding. Even I am surprised that I can fit in dessert after my dinner/breakfast and a hamburger for lunch.

"Um, can't," I say between chocolaty slurps.

"But you have to help me find a dress for the Fall Frolic."

Does she have to mention the dance? We have always gone to the dances together or stayed home from them together. This will be the first one that she goes to without me.

"I can't," I say. Right away I regret the snap in my voice. "I promised Grandma I'd do something with her."

"Oh," Julie says. "What are you doing? Maybe we could go shopping tomorrow? Mom had to cancel the spa."

"I have that medieval fair to go to," I remind her.

Julie's face falls, and I feel bad. I realize I haven't spent any time with her this past week because of Grandma Ann and my dress fitting.

"But let's get together tomorrow night?" I add. "After the fair. I can tell you how dumb it was. Maybe we can watch a movie?"

"I guess so," Julie says, and her face brightens. "And I can tell you the cutest thing that Danny said to me in French yesterday."

"Tell me now."

She grins. "Nope. And if you blow me off tomorrow night, I'll never tell you."

"Oooooo," I say, like I'm worried. We both laugh. It's good to be with my best friend. Maybe I'll even tell her about my eye surgery. But not yet. Maybe tomorrow night when it's definite and the surgery is all set. I don't want to jinx it now. And it's not like I'll have any cute Sean story to tell her. He's barely looked at me lately.

By the end of the day, Sean is the last thing on my mind. It's time for English. Usually I love that class, but today I'm dreading it. We have to present our scenes from *Romeo and Juliet.* Luckily I have a tiny part, but still, I despise getting up in front of anyone. If there's even one giggle, I always think it's about me. Julie says I'm paranoid. I say I'm astute (one of our vocab words last month).

As I walk into English class, I see my group staring at me.

"What?" I say as I plunk into a chair.

"Sandy has laryngitis," Vanna says. "She can barely talk, so she can't play Juliet."

I look at Sandy. She doesn't look sick. She does look bummed out, though.

"Maybe she can pantomime the part?" I say, thinking out loud.

Vanna rolls her eyes. "This is a tragedy, Lauren, not one of Shakespeare's comedies."

"Maybe Mrs. Hobbs will let us wait till Monday,"
I say.

"Already asked and answered. No way."

"That's so not fair," Matt grumbles.

"So what do we do?" I ask.

"Mrs. Hobbs said we have to rearrange the
parts, and we can use our books," Vanna says.
"Sandy can take the smallest part, because she
can talk a little before she starts squeaking. But
you'll have to be Juliet."

"What?" I say. "Why can't you be Juliet?" I don't
tell them I've actually memorized the whole scene.
I could even play Romeo if I had to.

"Because I'm dressed for the friar's part."

Only then do I notice Vanna actually is dressed
in a robe with a hood and a rope around her waist.
They obviously have a lot of strange stuff in that
secondhand store in the Village.

I look at Matt. He's doodling something on the
desk. If Mrs. Hobbs catches him, he'll be in after
school cleaning all the desks. He doesn't look much
like a Romeo, I think. Not worth killing myself
over, that's for sure. Like any boy is worth that.
What was Juliet thinking?

"So?" Vanna asks, prodding me with a black-
tipped finger. Not very friar-like at all.

"Whatever," I finally mutter. Like I have a choice.

I'm hoping we run out of class time, but there's a

good fifteen minutes left when it's finally our turn. By now my stomach is churning, I haven't heard a single scene before ours, and my hands are practically dripping sweat, never mind shaking like leaves in a nor'easter.

"And finally, the death scene," Mrs. Hobbs announces with a clap and a jingle of her secret bell.

I grimace as we march up to the front of the room to the "stage area" that Mrs. Hobbs has cleared for our performances.

"Hey, slant, don't you need your book?" Matt calls out behind me.

I want to die. Can the floor just swallow me whole, pretty please? "No," I say. My voice sounds squeaky and I know my face is completely red. I feel like I might pass out. "I have it memorized."

He looks startled for a moment, then shrugs. He says to Mrs. Hobbs, "Is it okay if I use my book? I, uh, don't have all my lines memorized. Most of them, just not all."

"Points off," Mrs. Hobbs says sharply. "Now stop stalling." She sits at a student desk, waiting expectantly.

We get into position. I literally can feel everyone's eyes glommed onto me. But then the strangest thing happens. I forget about my classmates and Mrs. Hobbs staring at me, and I actually become Juliet. I'm devastated when I wake up to see that Romeo

is dead. In speaking her lines, I feel her anguish at
being parted from her one, true love forever.

My part ends when I say, "O, happy dagger, This
is thy sheath. There rust, and let me die." When
I plunge the fake dagger into my chest, I hear a
couple gasps. Then I slump over Romeo, dead.

At the end of the scene, we actually get a standing ovation.

Vanna grabs my arm and stares at me intently.
"You were amazing," she says. The black around
her eyes makes her look even more intense. "You
could be on off Broadway. Really, I mean it."

"Thanks," I say.

"Good job," Sandy croaks. "Way better than
I could have done." She leans in closer. "And I
really didn't want to have to kiss Matt!" We share
a giggle.

"I kissed the air, trust me," I say. We giggle again.
Look at me, bonding with a cheerleader.

"Yeah, who'd want to kiss him with his big Jew
nose."

My giggles vanish like a popped bubble. "What?"

Sandy touches her own, perky nose. Her voice
is soft and raspy. "You know, he's such a Jew. His
nose is huge."

I look over at Matt, who is talking to Mrs. Hobbs.
His nose is kind of big, but I never thought of it as
having anything to do with his religion. In fact, I
never even thought about him *having* a religion.

"That's not very nice," I say, before I can stop myself. Actually, I have plenty of time to stop myself, but I let the words out anyway.

"Nice?" Sandy sneers. She's not so cute anymore. "Like he's so nice to you? Calling you *slant* and *chinko* and *gook*? You should call him a *kike* and see how he likes it."

She flips her hair and walks away. I can't move. I know *kike* is a derogatory word for someone who is Jewish. But like the word *gook*, I have no idea what it means. And now that I think about it, Greg Stankowicz is probably Polish. Everyone knows what a "dumb Polack" is. And Sean O'Malley is Irish through and through. Are his parents alcoholics?

I feel sick to my stomach. Everyone could be teased about something. Julie's super tall. Tommy Sullivan is the shortest boy in school. Nigel Obouie from Nigeria has the darkest skin I've ever seen. Even cheerleader Sandy has thick ankles. Okay, I'm pushing it there, but it's not like she's totally perfect, so why would she comment on Matt's big nose? Can't anyone just be a *person*?

te*n*

By the time the final bell rings, I've pushed Sandy, her thick ankles, and her comments out of my head. Maia has a play date and Grandma Ann is waiting for me at the curb in Daddy's old Subaru. She told him she had to run errands and needed the car. I race over to her, jump in, and buckle myself to the seat.

I've Googled the directions to the doctor's office, and I'm happy to see that Grandma isn't a typical old-lady driver. I'm a little worried about the cataracts fogging her vision, but cars are large enough to see, and I guess stoplights are bright enough to penetrate the film growing over her eyes.

We don't say much on the way. I'm too nervous, and Grandma concentrates on driving. By the time we get to the Surgical Center in Hartford, I can barely contain myself. This is it! This is it! This is it! All that saving and dreaming and wishing and praying. This is it!

Grandma insists we walk up the four flights of stairs for the exercise, which is fine with me. I'd be twitching with excitement in the elevator anyway.

At the top of the stairs, as Grandma catches her breath, she looks at me. "You sure you want to do this?" she half gasps.

"Absolutely!"

She smiles. "Okay, then, let's go."

The office is plush and quiet. The receptionist is pretty, and I wonder if she gets free plastic surgery because she works here.

"I'm Lauren Wallace," I say nervously. "I have an appointment with Dr. Sung."

"I see," the woman says. "Do you have your parents with you?"

"My grandmother. Um, my daddy, uh father, couldn't make it."

"I see," she says again, peering around me to look at Grandma, then she looks down at a chart. "Have a seat and the doctor will be with you soon."

We sit. The chairs envelope us in cushy comfort. There is an older man sitting in the corner, legs crossed, reading a business magazine. I wonder if he's here for a consultation or if he's waiting for someone. A woman sits at the other end of the waiting room. When she's called into the back room, I try not to stare as she walks by. One side of her face is all scarred as if she were in a fire. She turns to look at me. The other side of her face is beautiful. She actually smiles at me, but the scarred side doesn't move. But even with the scars, she still looks pretty, though I can't figure out how that's possible. Then she's gone.

Grandma reaches out and pats my hand. Somehow I'm not as excited as I was just seconds before.

"Lauren Wallace?"

I look up. A young nurse is waiting by an open door for me. Grandma and I go forward, and the nurse leads us to an office where we are told to wait. On the wall, a number of diplomas and certificates are framed and hanging neatly. They look official.

A little later, the door opens with a soft whoosh. The doctor strides in, not looking at all like a doctor. He looks more like an expensive car salesman, not that I know what one would look like.

"Hello, Lauren!" he says. He perches on the edge of his desk and leans forward to shake my hand. His hand is small and cold.

"And you're Mrs. Wallace?" he asks, extending a hand to Grandma.

"Actually I'm Ann Packer, Lauren's grandmother. Her father couldn't make it today."

"Fine, fine," the doctor says. "So, Miss Lauren, you want a double eyelid surgery as well as minimizing your epicanthal fold."

I nod. I've researched all the terms online, so I know what he's talking about.

"You're very young for plastic surgery. Can you tell me why you want this procedure?" He doesn't sound mean, but he's very to the point.

I squirm inside. I have so many great reasons, at least they seemed perfect until he asked me to say them out loud. I'd always said my prayers and wishes in my head. Saying them to Grandma had been hard enough, but this man is a stranger. But then again, if I don't tell him, it doesn't look like he'll do the surgery.

"I don't like the way my eyes look."

"I think they're beautiful," he says. "They look like mine."

Now I flush. Yes, we do have the same eyes. In fact, I remember from his website that he is Korean too. His eyes slant up at the ends, making him look like he's smiling.

"It's not that I don't like them on other people," I say quickly. "But at school I get teased. I look different from everyone."

"Everyone? There are no other Asians in your school?"

"Yes, there are some."

"And do they want this operation too?"

"I don't know. I just know what I want. I don't want to be teased."

Dr. Sung folds his arms, and one hand cups his chin so that a finger rests on the side of his mouth. "When I was your age, I was never teased about my eyes." His voice is softer now. "I was called shorty, shortstop, bug, teeny weeny. I begged my mother for anything to make me tall. Now they have growth hormones, but I'm pretty sure my mother wouldn't have given them to me." He laughs. "I'm still short, but no one teases me about it anymore except maybe my wife, but since she's shorter than I, she can't get away with it."

I figure he has a point in all of this. I wish he'd just spell it out instead of making me try to guess.

"Maybe I could say to you," he continues, "that the teasing will go away as you get older, or that it won't hurt as much, or that you should embrace your heritage and keep your exotic eyes." He pauses.

My stomach plunges. He's not going to do the surgery.

"However, I remember what it felt like to be teased. And although everything I just said is perfectly true, I do remember the pain. Therefore, if you have your heart set on this operation and you have your parents' permission, I will do it."

Tears come to my eyes. "Thank you," I whisper.

Grandma squeezes my hand. "Thank you," she

says, and I realize by her voice that she's as choked up as I am.

"Now," he says, getting back his business voice, "come over to this mirror and I'll show you what I plan to do."

Standing in front of the mirror, my eyes still shiny with tears, he points out what he will do with a scalpel for the *epicanthoplasty* and the double eyelid surgery.

"It could take up to a week for all the bruising and swelling to go down," he says. "But if you have no more questions, I'll let you make an appointment for the surgery at the front desk." He holds out his hand. When he shakes mine, I realize my future happiness is in this hand—the hand that will hold the scalpel.

At the front desk, the pretty lady looks in an oversized book. "Let's see," she says. "Believe it or not, we had a cancellation for next Tuesday. Would that work for you?"

I look up at Grandma.

She smiles and nods. "I guess I'll just have to extend my visit," she says.

And I can't help thinking how much easier this will be not having to tell Daddy until the operation is over. He'll blow his top, but it'll be too late.

"Since this is elective surgery," the receptionist is saying, "you must pay a non-refundable deposit now."

I was expecting this, so I have all my money with me. Grandma exchanged all the small bills for fifties and one hundreds before she picked me up. I gladly peel off the correct amount and get back a receipt. I feel like Charlie with Willy Wonka's magical gold ticket!

———

Saturday morning is a typical New England fall day. It's bright and chilly, with a few clouds racing across the sky. Shelley comes over early to help Maia and me get dressed. She's already dressed in a blue, velvety gown. Her hair is braided and wrapped on top of her head.

"You look like a princess," I say. The blue of her dress makes her blue eyes even brighter.

"A really old princess," she says, but I can tell she likes the compliment.

Maia and I get dressed in my room, and then Shelley pulls all the laces tight. Wondering if maybe last time I just imagined how great the dress fit me, I'm almost afraid to look in the mirror.

"Gorgeous," Shelley says behind me. "You look like an exotic princess."

"Me, too," Maia says, stepping in front of me in the mirror.

Little sisters can be such a pain. So I ignore her and smile at myself in the mirror. My eyes squint closed. I lift my eyebrows, trying to widen my eyes, but it doesn't help much. I try not to smile, but that's very hard to do when I feel all bubbly inside.

"I'll pull a bit of your hair back and make a braid out of it, okay?" Shelley asks.

I agree, and she starts brushing my long, black hair. Then she pulls back three segments of hair and braids them together, weaving a piece of green ribbon through it.

"Thanks," I say, when she's done.

"Me, too! Me, too!" Maia cheers, clapping her hands.

Shelley laughs and sits on my bed, pulling Maia onto her lap to work on her hair. Maia wiggles so much, Shelley can't stop laughing.

Meanwhile, I'm still standing in front of the mirror, admiring myself from all angles. I don't think I've ever looked this pretty. Too bad no one's going to see me. I think of calling Julie to tell her to run over, but Daddy knocks on the door.

"Are my three lovely ladies ready?" he asks.

Maia jumps off Shelley's lap, who is still laughing, and flings open the door. Daddy stands there, frozen. Only his eyeballs move from one of us to the other.

"Wow," he says, not sounding at all like a medieval lord, even though he looks like one with his tights and puffy shorts and shirt. "I must be the luckiest guy in the world."

Shelley takes his arm and squeezes it. "And we're lucky to have such a handsome gentleman escort us to the fair, right ladies?"

I nod. Maia has no clue and she's already skipping down the stairs to show Grandma her outfit and new hairdo.

Downstairs, Grandma Ann gushes over Maia and me. She was asked to come with us, but she said she'd rather stay home. She'd told Daddy last night that she was extending her stay for another week. I wasn't in the room when she broke the news to him, but I guess it went okay. Obviously she didn't tell him why. He'll find out soon enough. That thought makes me a little sick to my stomach, so I put it out of my head. For now.

It takes an hour to get to the fairgrounds, and by then it has warmed up and I don't need the suede jacket Julie gave me. The dress is long sleeved, and I am sure all the flounces will keep me warm. Besides, the jacket totally ruins the look of the dress, not that there's anyone to admire me.

Daddy gives me some money, says where to meet for lunch, warns me not to lose Maia, then tells us to go have fun. As he and Shelley wander off, calling "Good day" to Sir this and Lady that, I look around, wondering where to find the fun. Mostly it looks like a lot of people in weird clothes like mine, milling around.

I let Maia lead me. She follows her nose and we find the food stalls. I buy us each a caramel apple, and we crunch on those as we wander around. I've just thrown away our sticks and tried to wipe the sticky caramel off Maia's fingers, when she suddenly breaks away from me and takes off.

"Maia," I shout, "get back here!" I race after her.

She doesn't go far. She stops abruptly in front of a tall knight with red hair and freckles.

"Hi," Maia says.

The knight looks down at her and his eyes light up. "Hi."

I gulp. "Hi, Sean," I say. I cannot believe this. Sean O'Malley is here, at this fair, dressed in—in chain mail!

He's staring at me and hasn't even said hello. I look down casually to make sure I'm still all laced up, not that there'd be much to see if a lace had come undone—and then I remember that yes, there would be something to see! Or did I spill caramel on myself?

"Hi," he finally says. "You look really good."

"Thanks," I say, not able to look him in the eye, so I stare at his chest. "So do you."

"Thanks. It's chain mail," he says, probably thinking that's why I'm staring at it. "I made it myself."

"Really? That's so cool. How did you do it?"

As he explains how he made each small link out

of metal and attached another one to it, I forget to be nervous. Maia grabs both of our hands, probably bored with our talk, and pulls us along.

"That must have taken forever to make," I say, very impressed.

He grins and my heart just about stops. He is so cute. "It did take a long time. Almost a year. One of the guys at this fair showed me how to do it."

"Oh, so you've been to these before?" Duh! I mentally knock myself in the head. Didn't he just say that?

"Actually, I come all the time. There are a bunch of fairs all year."

"Really?"

Now he looks a little embarrassed. "Yeah, my mom comes, and she's been bringing me since I was her size." He shakes Maia's hand that is clutched in his. "She writes medieval books."

"That's awesome," I say. "Do you read them?"

"Not really. They're, uh, romances."

I stop, dragging Maia to a stop, who in turn tugs Sean to a standstill. "You mean she actually gets them published?"

He raises his eyebrows. "Yeah."

"Is she famous?"

Maia starts to pull us forward again and Sean shrugs. "I don't know. It's not like she's been on *Oprah* or anything. But she does make good money. She even has an online fan club. At least that's what she says."

"O'Malley," I say, thinking out loud. I like romance novels, especially medieval ones, but I don't recognize that name as an author.

"Actually, she writes as Candace Whitcomb."

"No way!" I squeal. I sound just like a piggy, but I can't help it. *"Candace Whitcomb* is your mother? I love her. I love her books! *Without a Prayer* was my favorite. No, *Dark Heart* was. But I loved the whole *Dark* series." I stop, suddenly realizing I'm babbling. Wait till I tell Julie!

Sean is grinning, but his face is so red that his freckles barely show. "Um, I'm glad you like her stuff. Do you want to meet her?"

"Yes!"

"Okay, she's signing books over there." He nods across the fairgrounds to a large tent. We head in that direction. "So why are you here?"

"My dad is a professor at Trinity. Mostly he teaches Shakespeare, but he also likes anything English and 'olde with an extra *e*,' is how he puts it."

"That's cool."

"Not as cool as you mother being an author," I gush.

"Is he Chinese?"

I blink. "Chinese?"

He must realize he's said something not quite

right, but he can't figure it out. He obviously can't even think of anything to say.

"I'm Chinese," Maia pipes up. I didn't even think she was listening to us.

"And I'm Korean," I say. "We were adopted. My dad is white. You know, Caucasian. He's actually mostly English. He says his ancestors came over on the Mayflower, and my mom used to say that they must have been stowaways."

He laughs. "Why stowaways?"

"I have no idea."

"Ask her."

"Actually, I can't. She died three years ago."

"Oh, I'm so sorry. I always say the stupidest things."

"It's okay, really," I insist. "How were you supposed to know?"

"Jeez, I feel terrible."

"Don't worry about it. Anyway, they couldn't have kids, so they adopted me and then Maia."

"So you're one hundred percent Korean?"

"As far as I know."

"I'm a mutt of German, French, and obviously Irish. It's cool that you're like a purebred. They're worth a lot more."

Am I being compared to a *dog*? I really don't know what to say to that. All I can think is that he is never, ever going to ask me to the Fall Frolic if he thinks of me as a purebred *dog*!

eleven

The next afternoon, I apologize to Julie for not getting together with her last night, but we didn't get home from the fair till after ten. Then I tell her all about meeting Sean there, and then meeting his mother. "She actually insisted on giving me her latest book, *Dark Promise*, for free! And she signed it. Look." I hold it out.

"For Sean's friend Lauren—a pleasure to meet a real fan! Keep the romance alive! XO Candace Whitcomb," she reads out loud, like I need to hear it again. "That is so cool!"

Then I pull out the extra book. "Look, I got one for you, too! I had to pay for this one, though."

She grabs it out of my hand with an excited,

"Thank you!" She reads this inscription silently, but I know it says, *For Julie—another romance fan—thanks for reading! Candace Whitcomb.*

"I promised Sean we wouldn't tell anyone about his mother though," I say, flopping back on the couch in her bedroom.

"Why not? I'd be bragging all over the place if I had a famous mom."

"I guess guys don't think having a mother who writes *romance* novels is cool at all. Maybe if she were a female Stephen King."

We talk about Sean a little longer. I don't mention his purebred dog comment. It's too embarrassing to share even with my best friend. Then I listen to her stories about Danny Sidowicz, and all the funny things he can say in French. I smile and laugh for her sake, but I honestly can't understand a word of the French jokes, which is why I now take Spanish after nearly failing out of French last year.

During our whole conversation, I'm dying to tell her about my eye surgery. I wonder if she'll be hurt that I kept such a big secret from her. I don't even understand why I don't tell her. Am I afraid she'll try to talk me out of it? That she won't approve and I'll have to defend myself? Whatever it is, I keep the secret to myself. She'll know, along with my dad, in a couple of days. Then I'll just stay home "sick" from school till the swelling goes down. When I go back to school, I'll have beautiful new eyes.

—

Monday after school, Grandma picks me up at the curb again. This appointment is almost as nerve-racking as going to the surgeon's last Friday. But this one is with a bra lady! I didn't even know there was such a thing. Luckily Maia has another play date. I can't imagine her running around the bra department!

Grandma pats my knee as I buckle up. "Don't worry, sweetie," she says. "Finding the right bra isn't rocket science, but it is important. And I called Victoria's Secret, and they have many women there who are glad to help out."

"Victoria's Secret?" I say, choking a bit. I imagine all the larger-than-life women I've seen in the ads. My boobs are matching pimples compared to theirs. "I don't think they carry my size."

Grandma laughs. I don't see anything funny. Then I have a worse thought. Victoria's Secret is at the mall. What if we run into Sean and I'm carrying around a pink-striped bag? Then he'll know I wear a bra. I don't want anyone to know I wear a bra except Julie, who couldn't come with us today on account of having a family therapy session that they have once a month ("whether we need it or not!"). This is all too, too embarrassing.

"Maybe we should just forget it," I say.

"Nonsense," Grandma says firmly. "There's nothing to it. I've been buying bras for years."

I have nothing to say to that. I take a quick sideways glance. Looks to me like Grandma might need a new, perkier bra. I just hope we don't run into anyone I know, especially *him*.

Luckily, we sail in and out of the mall with no problem. Victoria's Secret even has a bra that fits me! Surprisingly, I'm bigger than I thought. I get one in pink, one in white, and one in off-white. The pink one is my favorite. I even wear it out of the store.

I am floating like a balloon by the time we get home. I'm a real bra wearer (not just a training bra!), and tomorrow my life will change forever. I sweep into the house, only to find Daddy standing in the front hall waiting for me. His face is stiff and his lips are pressed so tightly together they are white.

"What is this?" he demands, shaking an envelope at me.

Grandma walks in behind me. Her humming abruptly stops.

"What is it?" I ask in a small voice. I've never seen Daddy so angry.

"It's from the Surgical Center. A Dr. Sung. What is it? What the hell is going on, Lauren?"

"Martin, keep your voice down," Grandma says. "You'll alarm Maia."

"Maia's still at her friend's house. Answer me, Lauren!"

Now I am shaking. I have never heard my father swear, not even say damn.

Grandma steps around me. I can see from her stiff back that she is shaken by his outburst too. "It's nothing to get upset about."

"I'm talking to Lauren," Daddy says, without even glancing at her.

"Daddy, it's . . . I'm getting a double eyelid surgery."

"What? What the hell are you talking about? Who gave you permission? Who put this ridiculous idea into your head?" Now he glares at Grandma Ann. "Was this your harebrained idea?"

"Martin, don't speak to me like that, I'm not a child. And don't speak to Lauren like that either. Let her explain."

"Then explain!" he thunders to me.

Tears well up in my eyes. "I just want the operation. I saved my own money. It—it makes my eyes less slanty. I—"

"Less what? Less *slanty*? For God's sake, what does that mean? Lauren," he goes on without letting me talk, "your eyes are beautiful. You can't operate on them. That's crazy! I won't allow it."

Grandma steps forward again. "It's not crazy,

Martin. The girl is unhappy. The operation will make her happy."

"Operations don't make people happy, Ann, and you know it. Was Charlene ever happy? Was she?"

"Well . . ."

"You let her get her nose fixed, but did that make her happy? If she was so goddamned happy, then why did she have to kill herself!"

The air is completely sucked out of the front hallway.

I get my breath back first. "Mom killed herself?" My voice is as small as a mouse's. "Didn't she fall and hit her head?"

Grandma starts crying.

Daddy speaks like a zombie. "No, it wasn't an accident, honey. She took a lot of pills. Then she did fall and hit her head, but she would have died anyway."

"You lied to me? For three years you lied to me?"

"I thought it was best."

"To lie? You always said that lying was the worst thing a person could do. But you are a liar." Now my voice trembles, and it raises in pitch. "You're a big, fat, stupid liar!" I know I sound like a baby when I am saying this, but I feel like a baby. A baby who has lost her mommy all over again.

Tears stream down my face and clog my nose. The top of my shirt soaks up the tears that drip off my chin. "You lied."

Daddy sags and rubs a hand across his eyes, under his glasses. "I am so sorry," he says. His voice cracks. I hear the tears in his voice as he says, "I really thought it was best."

"To lie?"

"I didn't know how to tell you. After Mommy died, I didn't know how to say anything." His voice catches in a huge sob and my heart squeezes so tight I think I'm going to crumple like a paper doll. "So I talked like a character from Shakespeare. I wrote notes to you. Anything to keep from having a real conversation with you. Anything to keep the truth from you." He's heaving with tears now.

I don't know what to do. I can't talk because my throat is full with anger and tears and fear. I've never seen Daddy out of control. Daddies are always supposed to be in charge. They are always supposed to do the right thing. To take care of their children. But does that mean lying to them?

I look over to Grandma sitting on the stairs, her large hands covering her face, silent sobs shaking her shoulders. I look back to Daddy, stumble forward, and fall into his arms. He wraps me up like he's never going to let me go.

"I am so sorry for lying to you, Lauren." He talks into the top of my head. "I couldn't talk about Mommy. It hurt too much. And I'm so afraid. God, I'm so afraid." He sobs and the shudder runs through us both. "I don't want to lose you and Maia. I don't want to lose you, too."

"Daddy," I say, my voice muffled against his chest, "I'm not going to kill myself."

Daddy half laughs, half cries. "God, I pray not. But I don't want to lose you to growing up. I should have let you have your ears pierced years ago, but I didn't want you to grow up too fast. I should let you wear makeup if you want to. But please don't let me lose you."

I squeeze him tighter around the waist. The anger and fear that filled me moments ago melt away like a snowman shedding layers in the spring. "Oh, Daddy, I love you. I'll never leave you."

Daddy's sobs turn into hiccuping laughs. "I'm afraid some handsome young man will take you away from me one day."

"Daddy, I'm only thirteen! You're stuck with me for a long time, so don't worry."

He pulls a handkerchief out of his pocket and wipes his eyes and blows his nose. I rub my face on his flannel shirt.

He cups my damp cheek in his hand. "Lauren, you are so beautiful, inside and out. You are an amazing young lady. Your mother would be so proud of you."

Grandma cries a little louder at this. I go to her on the stairs and hug her. Daddy hesitates only a second before coming over and draping his arms around both of us and squeezing us in close. I wish Maia could be here for this group hug, even though she wouldn't understand what is going on. I'm not even sure if I know what's happened. All I know is that I've just learned the truth about my mother's death, and I feel like a heavy blanket has been lifted off my shoulders. Did I always know something was wrong with Daddy's story about her accident? Maybe. Did I know he was outright lying? I don't think so. But now it's like a fresh wind has swept through the house, dusting away the old cobwebs. I feel lighter than I can ever remember feeling.

twelve

Later, Maia chatters all through dinner. She must love to have all the attention. Usually someone tells her to be quiet and eat, but not tonight. Her noise makes it easy for the rest of us to be silent.

We are sitting in the dining room instead of the kitchen. Daddy set the table while Grandma made baked chicken and heated up a can of corn. We usually eat in the kitchen, even when Grandma is here, so it's unusual to be in the dining room. Not really surprising, though, considering what happened earlier.

Daddy keeps glancing at me. Studying me. I pretend not to notice—pretend it doesn't bother me. But inside I squirm. What does he see when he looks at me? It's not as though he can say, *she has my ears and Grandpa's nose* or anything. Do I look like a stranger to him? Pieces made up of two people half a world away; people he will never meet. People I'll never meet.

He looks at my eyes. I keep my gaze on my plate.

"Shi," Maia says, cracking up. "Shi, shi, shi!"

I try not to smile. I know *shi* means *yes* in Chinese, but Maia likes to sing it over and over again.

"Me, me, me," Maia continues, clearly enjoying the rhyme.

I know what's coming next. We all do.

"Pee, pee, pee." Maia is giggling so hard she almost chokes on a piece of chicken.

"That's enough, Maia," Daddy says, sounding tired.

I know I'm not supposed to laugh when Maia goes off on her rhyming song, so I press my lips together. But Maia must sense that Daddy doesn't have the energy to send her to her room.

"See, see, see," she sings. "Shi, shi, shi, pee, pee, pee."

"I said that's enough!" Daddy barks.

No one expected that. We freeze. Maia's eyes flash wide, then fill with tears. She hops off her chair, her fork still in hand.

"Oh, God, I'm sorry." Daddy opens his arms,

but Maia doesn't run into them, she runs in the other direction. We sit in silence, listening to her feet pound up the stairs to her room. The door slams.

"I'm sorry," Daddy says to his plate. It's still full of food. So is mine.

Grandma gets up without a word and starts to clear the table. I guess dinner is over. I go up to my room, and as I pass Maia's, I peek in. She's playing on her bed with a set of tiny dolls. When she looks up at me, I see that the tears have dried on her cheeks in salty smears. Her smile is bright. Must be nice to be so young and forgetful, I think.

"Hiya, Maia," I say. I go in and sit on the bed with her.

"Hi." She hands me the doll with frizzy blonde hair.

"Hiya, Maia," I say in my doll voice. I mush the doll into her neck and make kissing sounds.

She scrunches up her shoulders and squeals. Then I grab her myself and make kissing noises into her neck. Now she's giggling. She throws her arms around my neck and squeezes as hard as she can. She either loves me a lot or she's trying to choke me to death.

I squeeze her back and my heart feels so big for her, all I can do is hold her. Tears spring to my eyes. She will never know how our mom died.

She doesn't need to know, at least not any time soon. Maybe someday I'll tell her, but maybe not. I mean, why does she need to know? Will it make her life better? How could it? If she asks me for details someday, I'll just stick to the accident story. I'll lie. Just like Daddy lied to me. Is that *lying for love*?

Maia wiggles to get out of my hug. She grins up at me, and her eyes narrow down to black slits. Her face is pie shaped, and her cheeks are so chubby she looks like an angel—all she needs is a pair of fluffy, white wings. Of course, sometimes she can be a little devil too, like when she took a purple marker to my favorite pair of sneakers.

"Play with me," she says.

"Not now," I say. "I have homework. And besides, Grandma is going to give you a bath as soon as she's done with the dishes."

"Goody, she makes lots of bubbles."

I leave her, and head to my own room. I actually don't have any homework, but the idea of playing with plastic dolls with their perfectly formed bodies, faces, and eyes doesn't appeal to me right now. I want to be alone to sulk.

Sulk isn't really the right word. I am numb. My dream has been destroyed, my wish shattered. As I dive onto my bed, belly first, I feel like I've wasted two years praying on a popped balloon. I bury my face in my pillow.

Now that Daddy has forbidden me to have the operation, there's not much I or even Grandma can do about it. Not at my age without parental consent. And while Grandma may have gone behind Daddy's back to help me, there is no way she'll defy him now that he knows.

Would Mom have let me have the operation?

How could someone be so unhappy that they couldn't bear to be alive? Romeo and Juliet had killed themselves over lost love, but that was just a play. My mom's life was real. And she didn't kill herself over lost love—she had Daddy and I'm sure he adored her. And she had me and Maia. Weren't we all enough for her? Didn't we love her enough?

I don't even realize I'm crying until Daddy's big hand rubs my back and I gasp for air between sobs. He pulls me into his arms and I cry on his shoulder. We rock back and forth.

"Why did Mommy do it?" I finally get out through my throat that's tight with tears. "Was it because of us? Because of me?"

"Oh, God no," Daddy says with a groan. He holds me tighter. "Never because of you or Maia or me. Mommy had a problem with depression her whole life. It was just the way she was made. When she didn't take her medication, life was unbearable for her."

"Then why didn't she take her medicine?"

"I don't know, Lauren. I just don't know."

"Why did she leave us?"

Daddy doesn't answer right away. I realize all this talking about truths must be hard for him after three years of writing notes and talking like a medieval character. "She didn't leave us," he finally says softly. "She left herself. She was trying to get away from herself. We were probably the only things that kept her here for so long."

That's a different way to look at it. To think that she might have killed herself sooner if it hadn't been for Daddy, and for me and Maia.

"Lauren," Daddy says, pulling away from me so he can look me in the face. "I've been thinking." The rest comes out in a rush. "You can have your eye operation if that's really what you want."

"What?" I jerk upright, ripping myself out of his arms. "I can? Are you sure? Why?"

He smiles, but it's sad. "You can, and I'm sure. Why? I have no idea what it's like to feel out of place because of something physical. Your eyes, your mom's nose—I never had to deal with that. I was teased as a kid because I was a nerd and I loved to read. But as soon as I joined the baseball team and pretended I'd rather watch television than read, the teasing stopped. So in a way, I operated on my life so I'd be more accepted."

"Are you sure?"

"Of course not. I don't think I've been sure of anything since your mother died. But I'm working on it." He tweaks my nose like he used to do when I was Maia's age. "Like I'm sure I love you just the way you are." When he sees me start to frown he says quickly, "But it's up to you. And I really mean that, Lauren. It is completely up to you." He gives me another big hug and then stands up. "Big day tomorrow. You'd better go to sleep now."

He gets to the door and I say, "I love you, Sir Daddy."

Turning and smiling, he says gently, "And I thee, Lady Lauren."

Once he's gone, the door shut behind him, I reach over and grab my mother's photo album. I'm tingling with excitement. With Daddy's permission, my dream is really going to come true. What would Mom say?

I open the album and slowly pour over every picture. Most of the pictures are just quick snapshots. Some are out of focus, or if anything is in focus, it's the tree way off in the distance. In most of the shots she's smiling. Do depressed people smile?

Then I come to the page where her nose changes. Maybe a neon sign would make the plastic surgery more noticeable. But as it is, the change is so slight, I still hardly notice it, even though I know it's there. Is that how people will look at me?

Will my best friend even be able to tell I had an eye operation?

I look through the album at least three times, cover to cover. Even though she is wearing different outfits, and her hair style changes, she grows older, and finally she has her nose straightened, there is something about all the pictures that is the same. Is it the color of her hair? Her white teeth? A feeling? I can't pinpoint it.

Finally I'm too tired to figure it out. I fall asleep, still dressed, on my back (it still hurts my ears too much to lie on my side), the picture album on my stomach. When I wake up, I'm curled up on my side, my right ear throbbing, and the album is wrapped in my arms. I don't move as I listen to the morning sounds. Maia is already up, jumping around in her room, getting dressed for school. She always insists on choosing her own clothes, which accounts for her weird color combinations. Her favorite outfit is her red and white striped skirt with her green and yellow plaid shirt. Oh, and pink sneakers. Ugh. Daddy is probably downstairs setting up the breakfast table with juice and cereal, and Grandma Ann stays in her room until after we leave.

I finally stretch. Today is the day. The big day. The day I have been dreading all quarter. It's the photography class critique day. No, wait a minute. I'm going to miss that! Today is the day I have been praying and saving for, for at least two years now. I jump out of bed. How could I have forgotten?

I shower and change. I thought I'd feel more excited, but maybe I'm nervous. When I'm ready, I go downstairs. Daddy is sitting at the kitchen table, reading the paper. He looks tired.

"Hi," I say.

He smiles. "How did you sleep? Did you sleep? Or were you too excited?"

"I slept okay." I don't say much else. I'm not allowed to eat anything so Daddy folds his paper and we get going.

We drop off Maia and then get on the highway, heading into Hartford. I pull down the visor and lift the flap for the mirror. Mostly I can just see my forehead, eyes, and nose. My eyes are deep brown, like dark chocolate wafers, my favorite. The bright morning light makes them sparkle. I smile, and though I can't see my teeth, my eyes narrow and they crinkle in the outside corners.

"That's it," I say out loud.

Daddy glances over at me. "What's it?"

I don't say anything, I'm just staring at my eyes in the mirror. They're still sparkling and crinkling. They are happy eyes. My mom's eyes were sad eyes. Even when she was smiling, her eyes looked deep and cloudy. And they didn't change after her nose operation. She didn't suddenly become happy. Her eyes were always overcast. Always depressed.

But not mine. My eyes are slanted, but they are always happy. Sure, sometimes they tear up, like they are doing right this second, and sometimes they cry like they did yesterday, but most of the time they reflect who I am, and I am happy, I suddenly realize.

"I am so happy," I say, turning to Daddy as I snap the visor back up into position.

"I'm glad, Lauren."

"No, I really mean it. I'm happy *now*."

Daddy looks confused. He peeks at me sideways. "That's great, isn't it?"

"Indubitably," I say, using a recent vocabulary word. I can't stop smiling. "Turn around. Take me to school."

"What?"

"I don't want the operation," I say, as if that's obvious. "I don't need it. I've just been—I don't know, scared, maybe. Scared to stand up for myself. I thought that if my eyes looked different, it would be easier to tell people to jump in a lake or something. But new eyes won't make me braver. Hey, a new nose didn't make Mom less depressed, right?"

"No, it didn't."

"I'm so happy, Daddy. The stupid boys who tease me make me sad for a few minutes, and they make me mad deep down, but mostly I am the happiest person I know!"

I'm still explaining, but Daddy doesn't need to be told twice to turn around. He's already off the highway and taking back roads to my school.

"Are you sure?" he asks.

"Yes!" I am so sure, it's kind of scary. Did I waste two whole years of wishing and dreaming after all? No way. It's just taken me this long to see clearly, no pun intended.

thirteen

"What is your problem?" Julie says. She stands in front of me, arms crossed, one foot tapping, head cocked to the side. We are in photography class. Our "portfolios" (aka manila folders) are in our hands. It's almost time to reveal our portraits.

"Nothing," I insist. "I swear!" I haven't been able to stop smiling all day. Julie isn't the first one to notice. It seems like everyone has been smiling back at me today as though it is my birthday and the whole world knows it.

"You're acting weird," she says suspiciously. Then a look of horror crosses her face. She leans down to me and whispers, "You're not drunk or high or anything, are you?"

I crack up and knock on her head, which I can only do when she's bending over like this. "Helloooo in there, anybody home?"

She glares at me and straightens up so her head is out of my reach. "Watch it, shortstop."

"Okay, Miss Jolly Green Giant," I say back. We both grin. We're allowed to insult each other.

Miss Shepard claps her hands from the front of the room. The bulletin board is now empty, ready for our critique session.

"I am so *very* excited to see your work," she gushes. "Who would like to go first?"

No one volunteers.

Then, to my horror, I raise my hand. What is wrong with me? I never step forward to be first, but there I am, with sweaty hands, pinning photos of Julie to the bulletin board.

The worst part is that Miss Shepard doesn't say a thing. She simply walks back and forth in front of the pictures, nodding, pausing, tilting her head this way and that way.

Suddenly she stops and faces the class. *"Well?"* she says, in the strongest italics I've ever heard. "What do you all think?"

I'm still facing the board. I hear nervous giggles and shuffling feet behind me.

"Julie looks like a model," someone says. I think it's this guy Tim who never says anything.

"Yeah, she looks really good," someone else agrees.

It's true that all the pictures I've taken look good. There is no such thing as a bad picture when Julie is the subject. But Miss Shepard makes us talk about light and shadow and composition, and by the end of my critique, everyone can see that though my model is beautiful, the shots aren't all that artistic.

But Miss Shepard says, "Good job, Lauren, and thank you for going *first*. Next?"

I thought I'd be relieved to have my critique over with, but I finally realize that it's the pictures *of* me that I'm most nervous about. I guess Julie is too, because she never volunteers to show her portfolio, and in the end, she's the last one. She looks even more nervous than I did. Her face is pale and I can see her hands shaking. Jeez, I'm not that ugly, I think.

The minute the first picture is tacked up, everyone stops talking. Even Miss Shepard stops pacing. I hold my breath as ten shots are displayed. I stare in wonder. When did she take these pictures? I never posed for them. That's it, I realize. They are not posed, like the rest of us. They are, as Miss Shepard gushes, *"amazing portraits of light and shadow, of mood, of reflection, of truth."*

I mean, I do remember sitting in the gym,

heart-attacking over Sean, but when did she take that picture of me in the bleachers? I look so fragile, like a porcelain doll, but at the same time, there is a strong angle to my shoulders and to the set of my mouth. What am I thinking? It looks like a moment before a battle, a mixture of reflection and determination.

And what about that photo of me cracking up? My head is thrown back, mouth wide (no wonder I eat so much, I can fit so much in!), eyes mere slits. But the way my hands are up and spread wide, the picture looks like it's moving, as though we can actually see me shaking with laughter, hear me even. It makes me want to laugh just looking at it.

Each picture seems to portray a different mood. It's amazing how much energy comes from every single one. It's like Miss Shepard told us at the beginning of the quarter about *capturing the soul of the person, the essence of the moment.*

In one picture, the last one, I'm staring right into the camera. I have a half smile and there is a strong shadow across my face so that one side is hard to see, but the right side glows as if I have a lightbulb inside of me. I can't stop staring at that picture. There I am, all of me. I see it so clearly. I don't have my mother's eyes at all. If anything, I look like the woman I saw in the surgeon's office with the horribly scarred face. Her eyes shone the same way mine do. And not to sound conceited, but it's breathtaking.

"These are amazing," Miss Shepard says in a hushed voice. And I know she doesn't mean me, the model. She means the photographer captured life in black and white and gray.

I'm standing next to Julie and I take her hand, giving it a squeeze. She squeezes back.

—

Right after school, I wait for Julie outside. I see her heading toward me, then I see Sean coming out of the building. I think I might wait for him too, but Matt and Greg are right behind him. Ugh.

"Let's go," I say, as soon as Julie reaches me. We are heading over to the kindergarten building to pick up Maia.

"Hey, gook," Matt calls after me.

I stop in my tracks. Julie whirls around, but I put a hand on her arm to stop her from saying anything.

Matt jogs up to me. Sean and Greg aren't far behind. "Yo. I thought maybe you didn't hear me. Did you do your math homework yet?"

"What did you call me?" I say.

Matt looks confused. "Slant?" The creep doesn't even remember.

"No, you called me gook. My name is Lauren. *Gook* actually means 'country' in Korean, which

I know because I took the time to look it up. Did you? The Koreans call themselves *han-gook,* which means 'Korean.' So you can call me *gook,* or *chink,* or *slant* if it makes you feel better, but don't be surprised if I don't answer." Sean and Greg are standing there by now. I'm about to turn to go, but I stop and say, "Oh, and I wouldn't give you my math homework even if I understood it, which I keep telling you that I don't. But your ears are so stuffed with—with—

"Cotton?" Julie offers with a grin.

"With stupidity," I say, "that you can't hear me. So read my lips. I. Suck. At. Math!"

With that, I grab Julie's arm and we march off. I feel great!

"Hey, wait!"

Julie tugs me onward. "Don't listen to them."

But I stop and turn around. I recognized Sean's voice. No matter how much I like him, I'm ready to give him a piece of my mind too. No more *lying by politeness* for me—or any other kind of lying for that matter. No more keeping words on the inside. I almost feel sorry for Sean. He hasn't met the new me yet.

He catches up at a trot. Matt and Greg are slouching off in the other direction. He looks between me and Julie, and says, "Ummm."

Julie rolls her eyes. "I'll meet you at the kinder-garten," she says to me.

After she walks off, I just stare at Sean, who is staring at his sneakers. I want to tell him that he hangs out with a couple of creeps, but he must know that already. And as cute as he is, maybe I should find a guy to have a crush on who has nice friends.

"Will you go to the dance with me?" he blurts out.

Now it's my turn to sound like an idiot. "Ummm."

"I know it's late to ask you," Sean rushes on, still inspecting his shoes, "but I was going to ask you a million times, I just was too—you know—nervous. I thought you might say no."

"And now you don't think that?"

"No! I mean, yes. No, I mean, I don't know. I'm still nervous. You might say no, but I hope not." He finally looks up at me. He looks like a beet, but it is the cutest beet I've ever seen, and I don't even like beets.

I try not to laugh, but I can't help smiling. It looks like he's not sure whether to take this as a good sign or a bad sign.

"Did someone already ask you?"

Then I do laugh.

"I'm serious. I heard that Aaron Miller was going to ask you before school."

"I got to school late today," I say.

Now he grins. "Good. Then will you go with me?"

As much as I like him, I hesitate. "Who would we go with?" I expect him to say Matt and Greg.

"I heard that Danny is taking Julie, so I thought we could go with them."

"That would be great."

"But there is one thing," he continues.

I just know the next words out of his mouth are going to be Matt and Greg.

"Uh, my mom said we have to stop at my house for pictures. You know, she gets all weird and teary about stuff like that. Probably 'cause she writes romance books."

I can't help smiling, thinking about having a picture of me and Sean. Maybe it's finally time to start filling up those empty picture frames . . .

But before I let my imagination go wild about a new dress and shoes, there's one more thing I have to check. Suddenly I'm nervous. The bravery I had just a couple of minutes ago seems to have vanished.

"Ummm," I start.

This time Sean interrupts me. "Look, Lauren, I also want to apologize for—"

But no matter what he's about to apologize for, I know it doesn't matter. He knows my name! "Yes!" I say. "I'd love to go to the dance with you, Sean."

"Really? That's awesome!"

We both laugh. He reaches forward, and before I know it, he gives me a quick hug.

"I'm late for soccer practice. I'll see you later, Lauren." He takes off, but he turns around and waves as I'm watching him.

I head toward the kindergarten, and I can't seem to wipe the smile off my face. To think, just this morning I was about to have an operation. By now it would be over. Would I be happier than I am now? No way. And that is no lie.

Laura E. Williams was born in Seoul, Korea, and adopted when she was one and a half. Since then she has lived in Belgium, Hawaii, Ohio, and Connecticut. Always an avid traveler, she has driven across much of America and Canada, visited Russia on a student/teacher exchange, backpacked through most of Europe, worked on a cruise ship in Tahiti, and lived on a sailboat in the Caribbean. Laura now lives in Connecticut where she teaches high school. With more than thirty published books, she continues to write every chance she gets.

More Children's Books from Milkweed Editions

If you enjoyed this book, you'll also want to read these other Milkweed novels.

To order books or for more information, contact Milkweed at (800) 520-6455
or visit our Web site (www.milkweed.org).

The Linden Tree
Ellie Mathews

Remember As You Pass Me By
L. King Pérez

The Cat, Or, How I Lost Eternity
Jutta Richter

The Summer of the Pike
Jutta Richter

Behind the Bedroom Wall
Laura E. Williams

The Spider's Web
Laura E. Williams

Milkweed Editions

Founded in 1979, Milkweed Editions is one of the largest independent, nonprofit literary publishers in the United States. Milkweed publishes with the intention of making a humane impact on society, in the belief that good writing can transform the human heart and spirit.

Join Us

Milkweed depends on the generosity of foundations and individuals like you, in addition to the sales of its books. In an increasingly consolidated and bottom-line-driven publishing world, your support allows us to select and publish books on the basis of their literary quality and the depth of their message. Please visit our Web site (www.milkweed.org) or contact us at (800) 520-6455 to learn more about our donor program.

Milkweed Editions, a nonprofit publisher, gratefully acknowledges sustaining support from Anonymous; Emilie and Henry Buchwald; the Bush Foundation; the Patrick and Aimee Butler Family Foundation; the Dougherty Family Foundation; the Ecolab Foundation; the General Mills Foundation; the Claire Giannini Fund; John and Joanne Gordon; William and Jeanne Grandy; the Jerome Foundation; the Lerner Foundation; the McKnight Foundation; Mid-Continent Engineering; a grant from the Minnesota State Arts Board, through an appropriation by the Minnesota State Legislature, a grant from the National Endowment for the Arts, and private funders; Kelly Morrison and John Willoughby; an award from the National Endowment for the Arts, which believes that a great nation deserves great art; the Navarre Corporation; the Starbucks Foundation; the St. Paul Travelers Foundation; Ellen and Sheldon Sturgis; the James R. Thorpe Foundation; the Toro Foundation; Moira and John Turner; United Parcel Service; U. S. Trust Company; Joanne and Phil Von Blon; Kathleen and Bill Wanner; Serene and Christopher Warren; and the W. M. Foundation.

Interior design and typesetting by Dorie McClelland
Typeset in Plantin
Printed on acid-free, recycled (100 percent post
consumer waste) paper
by Friesens Corporation